RELENTLESS

I found myself ahead of him in some appointed place, facing him, watching him bear down on me. I was terrified and unable to move.

The runner grinned.

I jerked upright, wide awake. The headache was back, roaring and drumming. I pressed my hands to my head, trying to absorb the agony.

He's coming, I thought. He's out there, some-where in the city, and he's padding toward me. He'll catch me unaware, and I'll be helpless . . .

Avon Camelot Books by
T.J. Bradstreet

DARKEST WISH: KITTY'S WISH
DARKEST WISH: LORNA'S WISH
DARKEST WISH: WENDY'S WISH

Avon Flare Books by
Jean Thesman

CATTAIL MOON
MOLLY DONNELLY
RACHEL CHANCE
THE RAIN CATCHERS

T.J. BRADSTREET is the pen name for Jean Thesman, who has written many books for young people. She is a member of the Society of Childrens' Book Writers and Illustrators and of the Authors' Guild. She and her husband live near Seattle with their dogs.

BEFORE SHE WAKES

T. J. BRADSTREET

AN AVON FLARE BOOK

AVON BOOKS
A division of
The Hearst Corporation
1350 Avenue of the Americas
New York, New York 10019

Copyright © 1997 by Jean Thesman
Published by arrangement with the author
Visit our website at **http://AvonBooks.com**
Library of Congress Catalog Card Number: 96-95266
ISBN: 0-380-78315-0
RL: 6.8

First Avon Flare Printing: July 1997

AVON FLARE TRADEMARK REG. U.S. PAT. OFF. AND IN OTHER COUNTRIES, MARCA REGISTRADA, HECHO EN U.S.A.

Printed in the U.S.A.

WCD   10   9   8   7   6   5   4   3   2   1

This is for my husband and the others
who heard me tell the story first.

Chapter One

I'm afraid to be alone.

I'm afraid to sleep. I dream of that man, the one I called the runner. When I sink into sleep, I know the same awful dream is rushing toward me again, and sometimes my muttered protests are so loud and I turn so restlessly that I wake myself up.

But other times I'm not so lucky and the nightmare falls upon me like a vicious dog. Once again I run through a ravaged and barren dream park, fleeing the footsteps that don't draw closer and won't fall back.

In my dream, dead tangled branches overhead form a tunnel. I race through it, and accompanying me are tiny birds, their hectic wings beating about my face, their terrified cries urging me on, faster and faster.

The runner calls my name. "Kate! Stop!" But my screaming mind flees through the park and down the street, where my sister Shelly waits for me. She doesn't see the runner. "Shelly, look out!" I yell.

But it's too late. He's seen her. He rushes past me, leaving me gasping in the wake of his evil, and hurls himself at Shelly. Then all I know is darkness and screaming.

My mother always wakes me out of the dream and promises me that I don't have to be afraid any longer.

She brushes back my short black hair and says, "It's all right now, Kate. Everything's all right."

But I can't believe her. I'll never believe her, because I know something she doesn't.

A few days after my fourteenth birthday, I flew to Seattle to spend the summer with my half-sister, Shelly. Dad, an archaeology professor, and Mom, who helps him write articles, were leaving for a ten-week journey through a remote part of India. The trip was really important to their work, and they were more excited than I'd ever seen them. But I'd traveled with them twice before, and I hated sleeping in tents or crumbling old buildings with lots of insects and no bathrooms. It didn't take too much complaining on my part to persuade them to let me stay with my sister.

Maybe they had more reason than my complaining about the misery of camping out in strange places. Maybe the problems I'd had at school made them think I didn't need any more stress for a while.

Anyway, they let me travel to Seattle to spend time with Shelly. She was twice my age—she'd been my first baby-sitter—and she was everything I wanted to be: confident and beautiful and smart and successful. And she'd said she wanted to get to know her little sister all over again. She hadn't lived at home since she went away to college, and she'd moved to Seattle last year, a thousand miles away from the rest of us. I could hardly wait to see her.

Shelly was waiting at the airport gate, just as she'd promised. She was tall and blond like her mother, whom I'd only seen in snapshots. Dad's first wife had

2

died when Shelly was ten. I was small and dark like my mother. Both Shelly and I had our father's blue eyes.

"You've grown taller since I flew home for Christmas," she said as she hugged me. "You're cuter, too, but I bet everybody's told you that. Come on, let's pick up your luggage, and then we can go home."

"I only brought one suitcase," I told her. "Mom gave me money to buy more clothes—she thought I might not have enough warm stuff for Seattle."

Shelly laughed. "Your mom's a California lady. When I first moved here, she called once a week to see if I'd frozen to death yet. I'll take you shopping for clothes whenever you like. It'll be fun."

Shelly had always made me feel important, even when I was a little kid. When I was with her, I forgot about being shy. I didn't stutter as much, either. My sister was one of those people everybody loved because she was so warmhearted and generous.

We had to wait a long time for my suitcase to show up on the carousel, so by the time we got out to her car, it was nearly eleven and I was surprised by how hot it was.

"I thought it always rained in Seattle," I said as we loaded my belongings into the trunk of her car.

"We keep this weather a secret," she said. "My apartment is in an old building, so it's not air-conditioned, but it never gets too uncomfortable. Buckle your seat belt and let's get going. I've got your favorite lunch waiting at home for you."

"Chicken salad sandwiches with black olives. You remembered."

As she backed out of her parking place, she said,

"I remember the rest of it, too. Double-chocolate shakes. We'll stop on the way home for them."

"Fun," I said. "I'm glad I'm here."

"I wish I could take time off so I could spend weekdays with you, but my assistant is on maternity leave, so I'm on my own until late August. But you won't be lonely, I promise. My best pal lives down the hall, and she has mornings off from the bookstore where she works, so she and her little girl will take you around town. You'll do plenty of swimming, too, I promise."

We stopped to pick up our chocolate shakes, and then Shelly drove us a few more blocks and pulled into a tree-shaded parking lot behind an old three-story apartment house.

It was an elegant brick building, with a steep roof and many-paned casement windows with stone ledges. At first sight, I thought that it was gorgeous, just the sort of place Shelly would pick. But then—I don't know—it seemed unfriendly somehow. I can't explain what I felt. But I didn't say anything to my sister.

"I live on the third floor," Shelly said as she pulled my suitcase out of the car trunk. "I guess this is as good a time as any to make my biggest confession. This building doesn't have elevators, so climbing up and down is how we keep in shape."

"I can handle it," I said.

"Well, well." A man had come up behind us and he startled me. "It looks like you've got company, Shelly."

He was barely as tall as Shelly. He was thin, and his freckled skin was sunburned, but it didn't make him look healthy, like an outdoor-lover. Instead, he looked oily and not quite clean. His nose was too big and his eyebrows were too close to his khaki-colored eyes. His thinning dark hair was damp with perspiration and clung to his skull. He wore a tee shirt, shorts, and expensive running shoes. I couldn't help staring at his ugly legs for a moment longer than I should have.

"Kate, this is Paul King," Shelly said without even glancing at him. She slammed her car trunk shut with more force than necessary. It didn't take a genius to realize that she didn't like the man, which surprised me. Shelly always seemed as if she could tolerate anybody.

"You didn't mention anyone was coming to visit you when I talked to you this morning," Paul said. His voice had an accusing tone, as if he expected Shelly to account for her comings and goings. "Who is she?"

He checked me out as he talked, glaring at me until I blushed. Then, apparently satisfied that he'd embarrassed me enough, he turned his gaze on Shelly. He smiled a fake smile, but she didn't look at him.

"This is Kate," she said briskly. "She's my sister."

His eyelids blinked rapidly. "This is the first I've heard of a sister," he said indignantly. "What's she doing here?"

Shelly didn't respond. She began walking toward the side door of the apartment building, and I trotted nervously beside her. She never acted this way! What was going on?

The man, Paul, followed us.

"I asked why your sister is here," Paul persisted. "This really surprises me. I thought that after our conversation this morning, you'd see that it's important for our relationship that you're always honest with me."

His voice had changed while he spoke, and had taken on a whining quality. He pushed between Shelly and me, elbowing me in the ribs, pushing me into a bike rack.

"Ow!" I gasped.

Shelly stopped. "What happened, Kate?" she asked sharply.

"Nothing," Paul said, before I had a chance to answer. He gave me a look I'll never forget. He barely knew me—and he hated me. "She got in my way a little and I guess I might have nudged her, but I couldn't have hurt her. Isn't that right, Kate? I didn't hurt you, did I?"

"I'm okay," I stammered.

"See, Shelly?" Paul said eagerly. "She says she's okay."

Shelly turned away from him and pulled open the apartment house door. "We'll see you later, Paul," she said abruptly, and she held the door for me while I scooted inside. She let the door close in Paul's face.

As we climbed the carpeted stairs, I said, "He was kidding, wasn't he? I mean, you don't have a relationship with him, do you? I didn't think I'd make an enemy before I even moved in."

Shelly shook her head disgustedly. "I'm sorry that happened. Believe me, any relationship we might have exists only in his imagination. He's an awful pest. I should feel sorry for him, but I've given up.

He just can't take no for an answer, so I'm doing my best to cut him short whenever I see him. Which is every time I stick my nose out the door, unfortunately.''

"How long have you known him?'' I asked. ''He doesn't live here, does he?''

"He lives across the street, in that new building. I've known him since last winter. He and Jack got into an argument in the parking lot once, around the time Jack and I were breaking up. Jack always thought Paul was crazy. But Jack was jealous of everyone, which was one of our problems.'' She laughed a little. ''Who in his right mind could be jealous of Paul?''

"Do you ever see Jack any more?'' I asked. Shelly had been almost engaged to him.

"Nope,'' she said. I was relieved that she didn't seem to care and hadn't been hurt.

Three people came down the steps toward us, a redhaired woman with a little girl around eight, who also had red hair, and a tall, teenaged boy with clear green eyes and dark brown hair that was longer than mine.

"Hey, this must be Kate!'' the woman said.

"Here she is, just as I promised,'' Shelly said. "Kate, this is Eloise McDonald, my very good pal,'' Shelly said. ''And her daughter Molly. And John D. Perry, who is our part-time handyman and the son of the people who own the building. Everybody, this is my sister, Katherine Williams.''

Eloise shook my hand and grinned. Molly offered me a bite of her apple, but John D. said, ''Don't touch that apple. She poisoned it.''

Molly doubled up her fist and aimed a sock at John

7

D., but he sidestepped and continued down the steps. "See you later, Kate." He looked back and laughed. "Molly, if you behave yourself, I won't tell your new neighbor that the other people in the building complain about your snoring."

Molly stuck out her tongue.

"I wish I could invite you two out for lunch," Eloise said. "But I've got to run over to the bookstore right away. A clerk is sick and Saturday's always the busiest day."

"I'm not going to my sitter's house," Molly said importantly. "I'm waiting on customers in the shop."

Eloise rolled her eyes. "Heaven help the book business."

"She can stay with us," Shelly began.

"No thanks," Molly said. "Mom needs me in the shop." She waved goodbye and ran down the steps.

"Thanks for the offer," Eloise said. "I'll do my best to forget your generosity before I'm ever tempted to take you up on it." She followed her daughter, calling back goodbyes, and Shelly and I climbed the rest of the stairs.

"Those shakes will be soup before we get to them," Shelly said.

"They'll still be good."

She unlocked the door to her apartment and we went in. I would have recognized it as hers anywhere in the world. Shelly was an artist, even though she worked as the manager of an insurance company. All her walls displayed her artwork—delicate watercolors and colored pencil drawings of wildlife and rainforest scenes.

"Unpack later," she told me. "Let's eat. I'm starved."

We sat at the table in the small dining room that overlooked a small patch of bright flowers. I saw John D. across the street, walking toward the door of the new apartment building.

"Does John live there?" I asked.

"He's called John D. No, he and his parents live on the other side of the park. They own both buildings, and sometimes John D. works in them part-time." Shelly laughed. "I don't know if 'work' is the right word. Mostly, John D. hangs around, chatting up the tenants. If you're ever curious about anything going on around here, just ask him—or Molly."

"Why is he called John D.?" I asked. "Why not just plain John?"

"His father is called John C. That's all the explanation I ever got."

I looked down at John D. again. He wasn't alone any longer. He was talking to Paul. From their body language, I guessed that Paul was angry about something and John D. didn't care the least bit. He walked away while Paul was still talking and waving his hands.

Way to go, John D., I thought, and I grinned.

After lunch, I called Mom and Dad to say goodbye one more time. Their plane would leave at 3:30 that afternoon. Then Shelly and I decided what we'd have for dinner, and she left to shop for groceries while I unpacked my clothes. I'd also brought half a dozen paperback books from home. I loved to read, and I'd never been able to decide if being shy helped me turn

9

into a bookworm or if it was the other way around.

My parents were glad I read a lot, but they weren't too crazy about the type of stories I liked best, spooky thrillers. I'd have been more convinced of their objections if I'd never caught them borrowing my books.

I stacked the books on the dresser and then changed out of the clothes I'd worn on the plane and into shorts and a yellow striped tee shirt. Shelly had a bike—she'd told me it was one of those chained up by the side door we'd entered—and she'd given me the key to the bike lock before she left. As soon as I finished hanging up the clothes I'd brought and loading the lunch dishes into the dishwasher, I planned on a bike trip around the park Shelly had told me about. I wanted to get acquainted with the neighborhood as soon as I could.

As I hung up my best summer dress, I glanced out the open bedroom window. Oh, yuck! Paul was standing on a balcony in the new building across the street. He'd changed clothes, and now wore tan slacks and a dark red shirt. While he watched the street, he shifted back and forth on his feet nervously, as if he was waiting for someone.

Then he looked up. The balcony was on the same level as Shelly's apartment, and directly opposite. Could he see me?

I stepped back, covered with goosebumps. Ugh. Did Shelly know he could see into her apartment?

I moved forward again and yanked the curtain closed. There, I thought. That'll show you that I don't want you looking in my window.

But I had this awful feeling that Paul could see right through the fabric.

Shelly's bike was great, much better than the one I had at home. I circled the block a few times, dodging the Saturday afternoon traffic which wasn't nearly as bad as I'd expected.

After I felt familiar with everything there, I turned north toward the park Shelly had mentioned. I rode through a neighborhood of tidy old houses shaded by tall maples and birches. Little kids rode tricycles on the sidewalks and older people walked their dogs on leashes.

I stopped at a stop sign, even though there wasn't a car in sight. Then I rode through the intersection, and ahead of me, I saw the tree-filled park.

Nice, I thought. Shelly had said there was a big goldfish pond there, with a fountain in the middle.

And then the car I hadn't seen hit me.

Chapter Two

⚡ I fell suddenly into a dark place shot with red flashes, and an enraged voice shouted, *"See what I had to do? See? See? Don't blame me for this. It was your fault. Your fault!"*

After a while the voice faded away and people talked at me but I couldn't understand what they said. My head hurt. My arm burned and throbbed. I was sick with terror.

Light came back abruptly, blindingly, as if I had stepped out of a cave. A face too close to mine said, "That guy must be crazy. He ran into her deliberately."

A dog barked and someone kept asking me where I lived. The dog barked again. I told the dog—or maybe it was a man wearing a shirt so white that it hurt my eyes—that I was living with my sister. "Tell Shelly where I am," I said. I could remember her phone number for a moment or two, but then I lost it because my head hurt so much.

Where was the man who had yelled at me? Was he still here? What had I done that made him so angry?

The man with the white shirt called Shelly on a cellular phone while I watched the dog take the lady away to report an accident. I insisted on sitting up, and somebody put a jacket over my shoulders.

"Maybe I should have called the paramedics," the man in the white shirt said. "Her sister's on her way, but . . ."

"She was able to sit up by herself," a woman said. "Maybe she's not hurt too much."

The light was too bright and my ears wouldn't stop ringing. Someone was talking to me, but I couldn't sort out all the words. Time passed and more time passed, and I was afraid I'd hear that man yelling at me again and I didn't know what I'd done to make him so mad at me. Who was he? Where was he? I was afraid to look around, so afraid that my teeth chattered.

"Oh, honey, what happened to you?" Shelly bent over me, frowning with worry, and I began crying.

"I want to go home," I said. I meant *home*, in Santa Barbara, where I lived with my parents. But there wasn't anyone there any longer. Even my cat was spending the summer with my best friend, Anne. Mom and Dad had left for somewhere—at that moment I couldn't remember where—and I was here in a strange place and somebody had hurt me on purpose.

In the emergency room, I tried to concentrate on what the doctor was saying, but my ears were still ringing, I was in pain, and I was embarrassed, sitting on the edge of a table in a cold examining room, wearing nothing but a skimpy gown made out of stiff blue paper.

"I can't find any broken bones, Kate," he said. Light reflected on his glasses and I had to blink because of the glare. "You've got an abrasion on your left arm and a bruise on your forehead, but I don't see any signs of a concussion. You'll be fine in a few days. The worst thing that happened to you is having the daylights scared out of you."

I tried to nod, but my head ached too much, so I stuttered, "Okay."

"Blah-blah-blah," the doctor told Shelly. His voice got lost in the ringing in my ears. "Blah-blah her parents, but blah-blah-blah."

"What?" I asked, bewildered. "What? I have insurance. Is that what you're talking about? You don't need to tell my parents . . ."

"I've got your insurance card, baby, right here," Shelly said. "Don't worry about anything."

"Bring her back Monday and we'll have another look at her, but I don't think there'll be a problem," the doctor said. He looked at Shelly, not me. The smile was for her, not me.

"I'll make an appointment on our way out," Shelly said briskly. "You'll give her something for her headache, won't you?"

"Sorry, but we can't do that," the doctor said. He smiled, as if that was the best news he could give me. "Pain medication would mask symptoms—if something came up."

"What sort of *something*?" Shelly asked quickly.

"Don't worry about it," the doctor said. He edged toward the door. "See you Monday, uh, Kate," he said. "You too, Shelly."

"Umm," Shelly said. She didn't smile.

The doctor winked and closed the door as he left.

"Jerk," Shelly said, and she sighed. "Kate, how do you feel, really?"

"I want to go home," I stammered.

"Good idea," she said. "Maybe you can't have any pain medication, but a cup of tea won't hurt."

"You didn't call Mom and Dad, did you?" I asked as I eased myself off the high table.

"No, because you made such a fuss when I mentioned it. Right now they'll be on the plane, but I've got their itinerary and I could call them as soon as they've settled down somewhere."

"No," I said. When I dressed and talked, my head ached even worse. "Don't tell them. You know how they are. They'll come back if you say anything, and the trip is a big deal for Dad."

And spending the summer with you is a big deal for me, I thought.

"We'll see," Shelly said. "We'll see how things go. Careful now. We'll go out this door—it's closer to the parking lot."

Outside, the light was even brighter and it brought tears to my eyes. "I wish I had my sunglasses," I said.

"Take mine," Shelly said, holding them out.

I groped for the glasses with my right hand—my left arm was stiff and bandaged from wrist to elbow.

"Who hit me?" I asked, suddenly angry and not stuttering one bit. I never stuttered if I got mad enough. "Somebody hit me from behind." Anger caused my head to nearly explode. I could feel my pulse throbbing in my temples. DRUM DRUM DRUM DRUM.

"Nobody got the license number of the car,"

Shelly said. "Or even a decent description of the driver. I talked to the police again while the doctor was examining you. They'll try to find the guy."

DRUM DRUM DRUM DRUM. There was so much noise! I put my hands over my ears, but I heard the drumming even louder.

"Here's the car. Get in, honey, and I'll take you straight home. If you're hungry . . ."

I groaned. The thought of food made me sick.

"Okay, no food. Maybe later. But everything's going to be okay. Don't worry."

DRUM DRUM DRUM DRUM.

I could barely think because my head hurt so much. And even with sunglasses, the sunlight stabbed my eyes.

"Be careful!" I cried when Shelly pulled out into traffic. There were so many cars, coming from all directions, with sunlight bouncing off them so that it was hard to see them, and Shelly seemed to be driving too fast.

"I'm watching everything," Shelly said. "Close your eyes and don't look. We'll be home in five minutes."

It took longer than that. I know it did. It was long enough for me to live over and over the moment when the car hit me. I hadn't heard brakes—he hadn't tried to avoid me. I'd only heard a woman scream, "No, no!"

Somebody had wanted to hurt me. That was the truth. Somebody had wanted to hurt me.

I went to bed as soon as we got home, and after a while I fell asleep. Twice I woke when the phone rang, and I heard my sister in the other room, explaining what had happened. The third time the phone rang, I got up and stumbled into the living room. "Don't tell Mom and Dad," I said, as if I hadn't already said the same thing a dozen times.

Shelly, sitting at the small desk in the corner, looked up at me. "I'm talking to Eloise," she said. "How are you feeling?"

"Much better," I lied.

I went back to bed and tried to make myself comfortable, but I couldn't fall back to sleep. Vague pictures and garbled voices arranged and rearranged themselves in my mind. I blamed myself for the whole thing. I shouldn't have gone bike riding until I knew the neighborhood better. I should have been more watchful.

Because nobody would really run down somebody on purpose. Nobody would *really* do that. I must have imagined that I heard someone say that I had been hit deliberately.

I heard Shelly coming down the hall toward my room, and I closed my eyes, pretending to sleep. I was aware of her pausing in the doorway, looking in at me, but I was too tired to talk any more.

Don't think about the accident, I told myself. Think about something nice, something gentle and sweet. Shelly's pretty watercolors or cute little Molly or laughing John D. . . .

Shelly went away and I turned over, trying to find a place on the pillow that was comfortable.

Shelly had no right . . . she had no right to do that . . . she should have told me . . . now look at the mess . . . I'm not going to put up with it . . .

My eyes snapped open. Who was that? I had heard a man's voice clearly. Someone was in the room. Terrified, I looked around as much as I could without raising my head. The hall light shone into my room well enough for me to see where the furniture was, but I couldn't see the man. Carefully, slowly, I raised my head and looked around. No one was there.

Was he out in the hall?

Did Shelly have a guest?

I swung my legs out of bed and left my room slowly, cautiously, looked for the source of that resentful voice. No one was in the hall.

"Kate?"

Shelly came out of the bathroom behind me. "What are you doing out of bed?"

"I thought I heard someone talking," I said. "I heard a man's voice."

"I left the TV on," Shelly said. "Sorry if it disturbed you. I'll turn it off."

"No, don't," I said. "It doesn't bother me."

I went back to bed, feeling like an idiot. That's what a really bad headache can do to you, I told myself.

I fell sleep and dreamed that a black car followed me wherever I went, even into a park, coming closer and closer until I could see a man behind the steering wheel, but I couldn't see his face.

"Go away!" I yelled in my dream.

He laughed and the car lurched forward.

I screamed and woke up.

"What's wrong?" Shelly cried from the doorway.

"It was the car that hit me!" I wept. "I dreamed about it."

"What?" Shelly almost tripped over the rug as she rushed to the bed. "You saw it before it hit you?"

I shook my head and the headache thundered DRUM DRUM DRUM. "No, I only dreamed it. But it was so real, almost as if I was remembering something."

Shelly sat on the edge of my bed. "If you think you saw the car, I'd better tell the police."

"I didn't see it," I stuttered. I felt like an idiot.

The doorbell rang and Shelly went to answer it. I shut my eyes and tried to remember if I'd seen or heard anything before the accident that could give me a clue about who had hit me. I drew a complete blank.

The little girl, Molly, poked her red head through the doorway. "Are you awake or asleep?" she asked.

She didn't wait for an answer, but came in anyway.

"I'm awake," I said.

"I brought you a sack of cookies," she said, holding out the sack. "There are only eleven. I had to try one, just in case they aren't any good."

"How are they?" I asked.

"Great," she said, grinning.

"Eat another one then," I said. I pushed myself up to a sitting position and leaned against the headboard. "I'll have some later."

Her mother came in, holding a paperback book. "Shelly said you like thrillers," she said. "This just came in the store. You haven't read it, have you?"

I squinted at the title, but the print blurred. "Thanks," I said.

"I've got another really scary one . . . Molly, leave

the cookies alone! How many times do I have to tell you?''

"Five times,'' Molly said, smacking her lips. "Or maybe more.''

I laughed, and it hurt my head. DRUM DRUM DRUM.

The doorbell rang again, and after a moment, Shelly brought flowers into the room. "Aren't these beautiful?'' she asked as she set the vase down on the dresser across the room from me.

The room was filled with a terrible smell, like rotting meat.

Goosebumps broke out on my skin. "Who sent them?'' I asked.

"They're from Paul.''

"I don't want them!'' I blurted. "They smell awful! Don't leave them here! Please!''

"Kate, what's wrong?'' Shelly asked. "They're only flowers, and all I can smell are carnations.''

Tears burned my eyes. "Give them to Eloise. Or let Molly have them.''

"No!'' Molly cried. "I don't want them either! I hate that man and I hate the way his flowers *stink*!''

"Oh, for Pete's sake,'' Eloise said, staring at her daughter. "Nobody likes him, but that doesn't mean there's anything wrong with the flowers. I told you to behave yourself if I let you come in Kate's room.''

"Throw them out, throw them out!'' Molly said.

Shelly looked helpless. "Kate? How about leaving them in the living room? You don't have to keep them in your bedroom.''

"Throw them out,'' I said. I had to work hard to

keep from gagging at the smell, which seemed to grow stronger every moment.

Shelly picked up the vase and took it out of the room. A moment later, I heard the apartment door open and close.

"She'll throw them into the incinerator," Eloise said. She sounded uncomfortable, and I was embarrassed. I'd acted like a lunatic—but I didn't want those flowers in my room.

"Maybe you should have kept them," Molly said suddenly. "You could have waited until the next time he was hanging around the parking lot, and then thrown them out the window and hit him. The vase was big enough to really hurt."

"Molly," Eloise said warningly.

"Well, *you* said you wanted to push Paul down the stairs that time he blocked your way and wanted to know where Shelly was and you wouldn't tell him and he got mad and you got madder . . ."

"What?" Shelly asked as she came in the bedroom. She looked amazed.

"I was already furious with him," Eloise explained. "He'd charged several books at the shop and I found out his credit card had been cancelled. He still owes me nearly a hundred dollars."

"The books he gave me for my birthday, I'll bet," Shelly said angrily. "Darn him. I'll pay you for them, Eloise. I wish you'd said something sooner."

"Hey, he's got plenty of money," Eloise said. "Or at least that's what he keeps hinting. Let him pay his own bills. I'll get after him one of these days, Shelly."

Shelly bit her lip and shook her head. "I wish he

were easier to ignore. Well, summer doesn't last forever. He'll be back in medical school soon enough and then he won't be around so much.''

"He wants to be a doctor?" I asked. The idea bothered me. Somebody that weird shouldn't be a doctor.

"That's what he says," Eloise said, and she laughed. "Molly and her pal, John D., think he's a liar, but I don't know where they get their ideas.''

I covered my face with my hands. "Can we not talk about him anymore? He gives me the creeps.''

"Good idea," Shelly said. "He gives everybody the creeps. Listen, people, am I the only one who's hungry? We didn't eat dinner and I bet you didn't either.''

"Molly and I will help," Eloise said. She gave Molly a gentle shove. "Come on, let's let Kate get some rest.''

I didn't tell them I wasn't hungry. The headache had killed my appetite completely. When I was alone in the room, I did my best to get comfortable and finally slipped into sleep and an uneasy dream, where I wandered in darkness and heard, in the distance, the soft pad of running feet.

Chapter Three

I woke late on Sunday morning, and for a moment, I didn't know where I was and I almost cried out. Then I remembered everything all at once—Shelly at the airport, ugly Paul in the apartment house parking lot, and the doctor at the hospital. I shouldn't have come to Seattle! If only I had the decision to make all over again, I'd have gone with my parents.

The pale blue curtain over the window kept out most of the sunlight, but it stirred a little, and I could smell freshly-mown grass.

The window was still open!

I sat up, alarmed, until I remembered Shelly's apartment was on the top floor of the building. No one could get in. I was safe.

Safe from what? Being run over again? I knew I was acting like a baby, but I couldn't seem to let go of the idea that someone had wanted to hurt me deliberately. Shelly had suggested once that the driver might have been drunk, but that didn't make me feel better.

When I got out of bed, I discovered that I ached from head to foot. My left arm, the one with the bandage, was stiff. I wanted to take a shower and wash my hair, but I wasn't certain I could manage on my

23

own. I bent to reach for my robe on the chair beside the desk, and my head throbbed.

"Are you up?" Shelly asked through the closed door. "I thought I heard you stirring around. Ready for breakfast?"

I was starved, and remembered then that I hadn't eaten for a long time. I opened the bedroom door and said, "I'll eat anything, as long as it's small enough to swallow."

Shelly laughed. "Hey, you must be feeling better."

"I really do," I lied as I followed her down the hall. There was no point in telling her that I was even more uncomfortable than I'd been the day before.

I slid gingerly into a chair in the dining room and drank the orange juice Shelly set before me on the lace placemat. The light streaming through the window was too bright, and I shielded my eyes for a moment.

"Your head still aches," Shelly said sympathetically. "Let me close the curtain."

"I'd rather borrow your sunglasses again," I said.

Shelly left the room to get them, and just as she passed the front door, someone knocked.

My heart hammered against my ribs. Who was it?

"Hey, John D.," I heard Shelly say after she opened the door.

"I brought Kate these," John D. said.

"Wait a sec and let me see if she wants company."

I was ready to say No, but Shelly seemed so pleased that I shrugged instead. When John D. saw me, he said, "Wow. You look like ten miles of bad road. I bet all your moving parts hurt, right?"

I stared at him, miserable enough to be resentful of

his cheerful smile and obvious good health. "I'm feeling a lot better today," I stammered.

He held out two video tapes. "These are funny and ought to cheer you up. I've laughed every time I saw them." The whole time he spoke, he kept his gaze on the platter of sliced melon in the middle of the table.

"Didn't you eat at home this morning?" Shelly asked, grinning. "Do you want to have breakfast with us?"

"I'm always hungry, but I've gotta get started on the chores around here," John D. said. "Listen, Kate. You'll feel lots better after you watch the movies and have a good laugh."

I took the tapes he held out and put them on the table. "Thank you very much, but I think I'll wait to watch them later. My head still aches."

"Oh, the sunglasses!" Shelly said, and she ran out of the room.

John D. sat down opposite me. "The bike's in terminal condition," he said as he reached for a slice of melon. "There's no way it can be fixed."

"I forgot about Shelly's bike," I said regretfully. "That's awful. Where did you see it?"

"I went over last night and got it—it was still on the parking strip. I left it downstairs by the side door. You're lucky you're not in the same shape."

"I *feel* like I'm in the same shape," I said. Shelly brought the sunglasses and I put them on. "Gosh, that's a lot better."

"Everybody in the neighborhood is talking about what happened to you," John D. offered. He took another slice of melon. "But when I went over for the bike last night, none of the people there could

25

agree on exactly what kind of car hit you and who was driving."

"You went around asking questions?" I asked, feeling a mixture of embarrassment and gratitude.

"Not exactly. One guy saw me picking up the bike, so he came out to talk, and then a lady came out of another house," John D. said. He wiped his fingers on his shirt absentmindedly. "He says the car was black and the driver was an old guy, but she says it was dark green and the driver was young. Everybody thinks he was either drunk or crazy."

"The police won't catch him," I said. Helpless anger tied my stomach into knots.

"I'll go crazy if I start believing that the driver will get away with it," Shelly said. "The police will find him."

I'd have been happier if she had sounded more convinced. "Maybe they'd look harder if I'd been hurt worse," I said.

"But you're going to be fine," Shelly said. "That's the most important thing."

"You didn't call Mom and Dad last night, did you?" I asked, worried again about how they'd react. After the problems I'd had at school a few weeks before, they'd practically hovered over me.

She shook her head. "No, you and I can handle this—unless you want to talk to them. They promised to check in once a week, so if you're sure you're feeling better, we can wait to tell them until next weekend."

I was tempted to ask Shelly to try to reach them, but I couldn't panic and give in to the awful feeling I had that someone had tried to hurt me. Mom and

26

Dad would drop everything and come home on the next plane, and I knew how important the trip was to them. I was all right, wasn't I? Only a lunatic would imagine that someone actually tried to run over her. Mom and Dad didn't need to come home.

But my vacation in Seattle certainly hadn't started out very well.

John D. only stayed for half an hour. Before he left he said that he'd come by some other time and see how I felt.

I was ashamed of myself for not showing more gratitude. "It was nice of you to bring me the tapes," I said. "I'll watch them, I promise. Just give me a while to sort myself out."

He had a nice smile. If I hadn't felt so awful, I'd have been glad for a chance to get to know him. But my head hurt and I wanted to lie down again, so I turned away and concentrated on finishing the last of my breakfast.

Later, Shelly removed the bandage on my arm so I could take a shower. My arm looked awful, with the skin scraped off and a nasty scab forming.

"The doctor doesn't want you to get your arm wet," Shelly said. "Do you think you can manage?"

I said yes, even though I was sure I couldn't keep my arm dry. What difference did it make? Water was clean. I was much more worried about my headache. My eyes didn't seem to be working right; sometimes everything seemed so blurred that I wasn't certain what I was looking at. But I knew if I mentioned it to Shelly, I'd end up in a doctor's office again—and explaining everything to Mom and Dad in person.

Oh, they'd come back, all right. After all the fuss

over ugly Bernina and what she did to me at school, they'd come back. I had to get well as fast as I could and not involve my parents.

Later, after I'd dressed in shorts and a tee shirt, Shelly put a new bandage on my arm and made up a bed for me on the couch. Finally I was in a mood to watch the tapes, but I needed to wear the sunglasses because the screen was so bright. John D. had been right. The movies were funny, and Shelly and I laughed out loud, even though laughing hurt my head.

While the second tape was rewinding, I went to my room to get a sweater. The sun may have been shining outside, but Shelly's apartment was too cool for me. When I passed my bedroom window, I glanced out and saw something glittering across the street.

I couldn't tell what it was. My vision was blurred again, but I could see something moving on the balcony across from me, the one I'd seen Paul standing on before. The glitter flashed again, then stopped, and I knew what it was. The person on the balcony had opened a glass door and gone inside. Had he seen me watching?

Oh, who cared? I grabbed my sweater and carried it back to the living room. Shelly was talking on the phone in the kitchen, and I heard her say, "Sure, any time."

"Who was that?" I asked.

"Your new pal, John D.," Shelly said, grinning. "He's found another tape he thinks you'll like and he wants to drop it off. He promised he wouldn't stay, unless you invite him. Of course, he'll do plenty of hinting about spending a few hours here. I'm sure he could convince his father that cheering you up is more important that sweeping the walkways or vacuuming the steps.''

I still felt pretty shaky. How could I get out of having John D. around?

''Hey, don't worry about it,'' Shelly said. ''I can tell by your expression that you aren't up to company yet. We'll just have a quiet afternoon by ourselves.''

I was lying on my bed when John D. came by with the new tape. I'd been trying to read the paperback thriller I'd started on the plane, but my eyes troubled me too much, so I appreciated having another tape to watch. But John D. was gone by the time I got out of bed and reached the front door.

''John D.'s a good kid,'' Shelly said. ''I see him with his friends once in a while, and they look like they'd be fun for you. I'm sure he'll introduce you around as soon as you feel better.''

I nodded. Making friends was a lot easier when you had somebody like John D. doing most of the work. He didn't seem a bit shy.

Shelly made lemonade and we watched the new tape together. I had trouble staying awake—I'd never watched three tapes in one day before—and finally Shelly laughed and told me I ought to quit fighting it and take a nap.

''I'll pick up some takeout food for an early dinner and wake you up when I get back,'' she said. ''What sounds good to you?''

''Pizza,'' I said.

''And a big salad,'' she said as she took her purse out of the small closet by the front door. ''You sleep for a while and then we'll eat. And maybe this evening we can go out for double-chocolate ice cream with Eloise and Molly.''

After she left, I tried to get comfortable in my room, but I didn't feel sleepy any longer. I got up to get a drink of water, and the apartment seemed cold and strange. I wished I had gone with Shelly. Instead of returning to my room, I lay down on the couch and waited.

I couldn't bear the silence, so I put John D.'s tape back into the VCR and tried to concentrate on it. I couldn't. I kept going over and over the conversation I'd had with my parents when I told them I honestly didn't want to spend weeks with them crawling around in old ruins and sleeping in places that didn't have indoor plumbing. I wanted to spend time with my big sister in a city I didn't know very much about.

If I'd gone with Mom and Dad, I wouldn't have been run down by somebody who was drunk or crazy.

I heard voices in the hall and I sat up straight. Shelly came in with a tall, dark-haired man with a nice smile. He carried a pizza box and Shelly held a plastic container of green salad.

''Hi, Kate,'' the man said. ''I hope we didn't wake you up, barging in like this.''

Shelly introduced him as Andy James, who worked in the same office building with her. I could tell he liked Shelly a lot—and he seemed so friendly and nice that I hoped she liked him, too.

Shelly had set the table before she left, so we sat down and began eating. Andy asked all the right questions, the kind that make a stranger feel good, and I found myself talking more about myself than I usually did.

"You're a lot like your sister," Andy told me. "I like women with a sense of humor."

Shelly's fair skin turned pink. She's attracted to him, I thought. Good.

Andy didn't stay late—he said he didn't want to tire me out—and Shelly walked downstairs with him to say goodbye. I felt restless, so I began clearing the table, and I glanced out the window in time to see the glass door on the balcony across the street close.

My heart skipped a beat.

I closed the curtain quickly and finished clearing the table. When the phone rang, I jumped, and for a moment, I didn't want to answer it. But after four rings, I picked it up and said hello.

"Hey, did you like the tapes?"

I recognized John D.'s voice. "They were great," I said. "Thanks a lot."

"Is it too late to come by and pick them up?" he asked. "Since you're finished with them, I'll take them back to the rental place."

I told him it wasn't too late, and said goodbye. I couldn't help smiling.

Shelly came in as I hung up. "Who was that?" she asked.

"John D. wants to pick up the tapes," I told her.

"Good, good," she said, but I didn't think she was really paying attention to what we were talking about. I suspected she was thinking about Andy.

The doorbell rang. "John D.'s here so soon?" Shelly asked. She opened the door.

Paul darted in. I clamped my hand over my mouth and backed up a step.

"Who was the guy you were with?" Paul asked

Shelly quickly, urgently. *You have no right, you have no right, who is he, what did he want, did you let him touch you, kiss you . . .*

I heard his garbled, furious thoughts as loudly as though he had shouted them! I actually knew what he was thinking! This scared me so much that I backed up another step.

"For heaven's sake, what business is it of yours?" Shelly asked Paul sharply.

Paul had been trying to close the door behind him, but Shelly blocked him. My head throbbed and I felt half sick from the power of his thoughts.

"I didn't like his looks," Paul whined. "How do you know you can trust him?" *You think he's good-looking, you don't care that he's stupid . . .* "You shouldn't bring home strangers. You don't know what might happen."

"He's not a stranger," Shelly snapped. "I've known him for months, not that I need to explain anything to you. We don't want any more company tonight, Paul. You'll have to leave, right now."

"I worry about you, and wanted to make sure you were all right," he said. He smiled, but the smile didn't reach his eyes. *I'll get even, Shelly. I'll pay you back. First you put this girl between us, and then this man. I saw how you laughed with him. You'd been talking about me and laughing at me. At me, me, me . . .*

Paul had watched us all through dinner, I thought. He could have seen us clearly from his windows, since we had turned on the swag light over the table.

"Well, you can see that we're just fine," Shelly

said briskly. "Step back, Paul. I need to close the door now."

He didn't back up. Instead, he turned his tan eyes toward me. "Did you like the flowers, Kate?" he asked.

I'd forgotten about them. I didn't know what to say. The truth—that I'd wanted them thrown away—might anger him, and I didn't want to do anything that would fix his attention on me again.

"Kate's allergic to flowers, but she did enjoy seeing them before I had to remove them so they wouldn't make her sick," Shelly said smoothly. "Excuse me, Paul, but I really must close the door."

I wasn't quite certain how she managed it, but she succeeded in backing him out through the open door. "Goodnight," she said, and she shut the door firmly.

"Oh, Shelly," I said, and my voice shook with fright.

"He's repulsive," she said. "I wish I'd never tried being nice to him. He takes advantage . . ."

"Hey, knock it off!" someone in the hall shouted.

Shelly yanked open the door before I could protest. "John D., are you okay?" she called out.

John D. came in, rubbing his arm. "Jeez, I hate Paul," he said, looking back over his shoulder. "He knocked me into the wall and pretended it was an accident."

Accident.

Shelly sighed. "Paul has all the charm of a garden slug," she said, and both John D. and I laughed.

John D. picked up the tapes, switched them from hand to hand, and looked around. "Everything okay here?" he asked. He looked straight at me. "You okay? A couple of the girls living in the other building are afraid of Paul, especially after what happened to Suzanne's birds.''

''What birds?'' I asked.

''She—Suzanne, I mean—came home and found that somebody had killed all her finches. She had them out on her balcony.''

''Weren't they in a cage?'' Shelly asked.

''Sure,'' John D. said. ''She had a big cage for them. They were neat little guys. Anyway, all of them were dead, with broken necks, and she said she was sure Paul had done it because he hated them being out on the balcony where he could hear them. Her balcony is right next to his.''

Shelly made a face. ''That's horrible. Did she call the police?''

''Yeah, but they didn't do anything about it. I mean, nobody saw the creep killing the birds, so it was her word against his. At least, that's what Suzanne told my parents when she asked them to evict Paul.''

''But they didn't,'' I said. My voice was nearly a whisper.

''He's got a lease,'' John D. said. ''My mom can't stand him, but there wasn't anything she and Dad could do. He threatened to sue them if they didn't stop asking him to leave. His father's a lawyer.''

There'll never be anything anybody can do, I thought. Not about him. He's like a school bully. They always manage to get away with everything.

''So Suzanne's lease is up next month and she's moving,'' John D. finished.

"I don't blame her," Shelly said. "It sounds like he's a lot of trouble for your family."

"It's always something with him," John D. said. "His faucets drip, his windows are drafty, his doors stick. Gripe, gripe, gripe. Hey, enough about him. Kate, you want to go to the aquarium tomorrow?"

"Let's hold off on that," Shelly said. "Kate's still not feeling all that great."

I hadn't had a chance to answer for myself. I'd have wanted to ask for a raincheck, if I'd had the courage. But Shelly was right. I still didn't feel very well.

"Maybe another time," I finally managed to stammer.

John D. grinned down at me. "Great," he said. "Well, ladies, I'll see you later. Maybe I can catch up with Paul and knock him down the stairwell." He ran off laughing before Shelly and I could respond.

Shelly shut the door and fastened the chain. I hoped that it was an automatic gesture and not because she was worried about Paul coming back.

"You look worn out," Shelly said. "How are you feeling? Honestly?"

"I'm tired, and my arm is sore," I told her. "Bed sounds pretty good to me."

"Goodnight, then, Katie," my sister said, and she hugged me gently. "This was a busier evening than I'd planned for you. Sorry."

"I'll be fine," I said.

I went down the hall by myself and I was careful to leave my bedroom door ajar. I didn't want to feel alone.

I didn't want to *be* alone.

In the dark.

I changed into my pajamas, turned out my light, and crawled into bed. But I could hear a voice in my mind, muttering, whispering.

You're in the way, Kate. I don't want you in Seattle. You'd better leave. Everything's your fault. The guy wouldn't have been with Shelly tonight if it hadn't been for you.

I don't want you staying with Shelly.

I want you gone, one way or another.

I'll succeed—next time.

Chapter Four

The dream rushed at me.

I ran through a bare and ravaged park, fleeing the footsteps that had pursued me for so long I couldn't remember anything else. Bare branches whipped me. Overhead, tiny birds fled in terror.

The formless pursuer called my name sharply, demanding that I stop. My legs wanted to obey—I was so tired!—but my screaming mind fled beneath the twisted, leafless trees, and the footsteps followed, followed, and then the birds were gone and I was out of the park, running on the street, unable to breathe because the pain in my chest was so bad.

Ahead, I saw Shelly. "Run, Shelly!" I screamed. "He can see you! He knows you're here!"

The runner passed me, shouting with laughter. Somewhere, far away, I heard my sister scream, once.

I sat up, fully awake in the dark, out of breath, gasping and choking. I could still hear the runner's footsteps.

Suddenly, in my mind, I saw the inside of a brightly-lighted room. It was nearly bare, containing only a bed, a chair, and a table. Curtains covered the window. Photographs covered the walls.

In my mind, I tried to get closer to the photographs

so that I could identify the person in them. She was blond—that much I knew. But I couldn't see the face clearly. Not yet, anyway. Not yet, but . . .

Shelly rapped lightly on the door and called my name.

I nearly screamed. "I'm awake," I said hoarsely. My strange vision vanished as soon as I spoke.

Shelly opened the door and slipped in. The hall light shone behind her and I recognized her outline, but still, my heart seemed to turn over. I reached for the bedside light and turned it on.

"You must have been having a nightmare," she said as she sat beside me on the bed. "I heard you cry out."

I wanted to shout, "No! It was you who cried out—because the runner caught you!" But I knew I had been dreaming and so I said, "Sorry I woke you."

"I was reading in bed," she said. She brushed back my bangs. "Your skin is icy cold. I'll get you another blanket."

She took one off the top shelf of my closet and spread it over me, tucking it under the edge of the mattress as if I were a small child.

"You going to be okay now?" she asked.

"Sure," I said. My heart was beating so hard I hoped she couldn't hear it. "I'll be fine. I'm sorry I bothered you."

"You didn't bother me, not at all. Did you have a nightmare about the accident? I wouldn't blame you if you did. I'd have nightmares for a month if a car had knocked me off a bike."

She didn't seem to expect an exact answer to her question about my dream, and I was grateful. I didn't want to tell her. I didn't want to describe it to her and make it seem real—and maybe give it a chance to come true.

"I'll call the police again as soon as I get to my office in the morning," Shelly went on. "Maybe they know something about the car. At least I want them to understand that we aren't going to let this go. The man should be punished for hitting you and driving away. I get sick all over when I think about what might have happened to you."

"I'd feel better if he was caught," I said. I lay back down and pulled both blankets up to my chin. "You should get some sleep," I told her. "You have to work tomorrow."

"Maybe I won't go into the office," she said. She bit her lower lip and frowned. "Maybe I'll . . ."

"No, go to work," I said. "I'll be fine. I'll watch TV and read."

"Then I'll call home every two hours," she said. "I'll be pestering you, but at least I'll feel better. Goodnight, and try to get back to sleep and dream something nice this time. Okay?"

"Okay," I said, and I did my best to smile.

I knew I wouldn't fall asleep very soon. I didn't want to dream that dream again. But what had happened afterward—the room I'd seen in my mind—hadn't been part of the dream. I had *seen* that room.

His room.

The dream runner's room.

I left the bedside light on, and tried to sort out what was happening to me. Were my nightmares connected to the accident? Or was it a combination of being injured and staying in a building that seemed creepy to me?

Oh, it was a beautiful apartment house, all right. But it reminded me of the buildings in the spooky books I liked to read—all that dark brick and ivy, and the small-paned windows, and the high ceilings.

How many times had Mom told me I ought to give up reading thrillers? Only about a million, I guessed.

I don't know when I fell asleep again. At least I didn't dream.

I took a shower before Shelly left for work so that she could change the bandage on my arm. The scrape seemed to be healing so it really didn't need to be covered any longer, but it was ugly and I wanted to hide it.

After Shelly left, I turned the TV on, drank another glass of juice, and made myself comfortable on the couch with a pillow from my bed. There was a stack of new magazines on the coffee table, and I paged through a few slowly.

But I couldn't concentrate. My head still ached, although not as much as it had when I woke up from that nightmare.

I told myself I'd feel better as soon as the police caught the man who hit me. Then I'd quit having nightmares and my imagination would stop tormenting me. The fun I expected to have staying in Seattle with my sister would finally begin.

Time dragged. Shelly called a few minutes before ten, to ask how I was and tell me that the police didn't know any more than they had before about the car that had hit me.

"But they haven't given up," she said. "The man I spoke to assured me of that. It's only been a couple of days."

It seemed like a couple of years to me. Shelly promised to call back at noon, and then she asked me again how I was feeling.

"Fine," I said. "Honestly."

I said goodbye before she could question me anymore.

At ten o'clock, the doorbell rang. I would have jumped out of my skin if I hadn't heard Molly's voice out in the hall.

"Let me do it, Mom!" she said. "I want to do it. Let me tell Kate."

I opened the door and found the little girl and her mother waiting there, dressed in matching blue tee shirts, shorts, and sneakers.

"We look nice in our new clothes, don't we?" Molly demanded. "We're going to the bakery and then we're going to spend lots of time at the toy store. You want to come, don't you?"

Eloise gently rapped her daughter's head with a knuckle. "Ask, don't tell, Molly," she said. "Excuse her, Kate. She thinks everybody wants what she wants. We're also going to the drugstore and the fruit-and-vegetable market, whether she wants to or not. Do you feel up to going along?"

"I'd love to, but I'd better call Shelly first," I said.

I called the number Shelly had taped to the wall next to the kitchen phone, but a brisk-voiced woman told me Shelly was in a meeting and couldn't be disturbed. I left a message, explaining that I was going out with the neighbors, but the woman didn't sound very interested and I had an uneasy feeling that maybe she wouldn't bother to tell Shelly.

"Probably I shouldn't stay out too long," I told Eloise. "I don't want to worry my sister."

"What a nice kid you are!" Eloise said. "Molly doesn't bother me with information about her whereabouts, since she thinks I can read minds."

Molly stared at her. "Well, *I* can read minds. I can always tell what you're thinking."

Eloise grinned. "If that were true, you wouldn't be bragging about it right at this exact moment, kiddo."

I found the key Shelly had given me, and locked the deadbolt behind us when we went out. I hoped the lock was a secure one. A sudden chill brought goosebumps up on my bare arms—and I saw Molly looking up at me in surprise.

"Nobody can get in," she said.

Maybe she *could* read minds.

When we started down the steps, Molly began counting until Eloise made her stop.

"It's not as if I don't know exactly how many stairs there are, Molly," she said. "You've been counting them—and *counting* them—so long that everybody in the whole building knows."

Molly went on counting, as if Eloise had never spoken. I couldn't help grinning. She was a sassy child and I envied her, but she must have been a handful.

I forgot about my aches and pains while we walked to the neighborhood shopping district. Molly and her mother were good company, and I found myself laughing a lot. We were gone for only a little over an hour, which relieved my worry about Shelly calling and finding me gone.

Molly counted the stairs going back up, too. But I didn't pay much attention, because Eloise was telling me how much she disliked Shelly's old boyfriend and how much she liked Andy. Shelly had introduced her to Andy when Shelly walked him out to his car.

As we left the last landing to head up the last of the stairs, I heard a dry flutter over my head and looked up, expecting to see a bird trapped inside the building. But nothing was there. Goosebumps broke out on my arms again.

And then I realized that Molly had quit counting and was looking up, too, while her mother went on talking about how nice Andy had seemed.

Molly and I exchanged a look, but she didn't say a word.

She heard the sound and she's afraid, I thought. And so am I.

"We have to be careful," Molly told me.

"What?" her mother asked. "Well, of course we should be careful on these stairs."

But that wasn't what Molly had meant. The dry flutter of invisible feathers had been a warning.

The birds in my nightmare had been warning me, too.

Molly resumed counting and I burst out laughing nervously. Hadn't she lost count while she and I were letting each other know we understood what had happened? My own mind was so rattled and confused that I don't think I could have remembered my age.

At the top of the stairs, Eloise and Molly turned left toward their own apartment and I turned right toward Shelly's. I fished out my key and unlocked the door—and then stood very still, listening. The apartment was silent. I stepped inside, but I didn't shut the door at first.

I had the strange feeling that the phone had just stopped ringing. The air seemed almost electrified.

Without closing the door, I walked slowly across the living room toward the kitchen. I could see the answering machine on the counter. The light wasn't blinking, so there hadn't been a call. At least, no one had left a message.

But the ringing had disturbed the place somehow, and I could feel it.

Stop it, I told myself. I was scaring myself.

My headache came back and hurt worse than ever.

When Shelly called, I asked her if she'd received my message. She had, but she didn't sound too happy about it.

"I wish you wouldn't go anywhere unless you've talked to me," she said. "I can tell from your voice that you're not feeling very well. It's a good thing I called my own doctor and made an appointment for you at 4:30, because I want a second opinion on your injuries. Those headaches—they shouldn't be so bad."

"I bumped my head when I fell off the bike," I said. "That would make anybody's head ache."

"But the doctor in the emergency room said you didn't have a concussion," Shelly said. "Let's wait to see what *my* doctor says. Okay?"

What could I do but agree?

"I left a sandwich for you in the refrigerator . . ." she went on.

"I remember," I said.

I guess I sounded cranky, because she said, "I know you remember. I guess I'm trying to take your mother's place. Eat your lunch and lie down for a nap. I'll come home early and take you to Dr. Francis. You'll like her—and I trust her. I should have called her right at the start instead of taking you to the emergency room."

"I'll be okay," I said. "Stop worrying. I'm going to eat now and then lie down. See you later."

I sighed with relief when I hung up. My head was pounding hard—but I didn't want Shelly or her doctor to know. I didn't want anything to be wrong with me. If I had a concussion, maybe that would account for my nightmares and the feeling I had that I could read the mind of the man who hit me and even knew what his room looked like.

But didn't those things also mean I was probably crazy?

If I had a head injury—if maybe I . . .

I couldn't stand to think about it. I didn't know anything about head injuries except for a few things I'd seen on TV—people paralyzed, unable to speak, blind and deaf.

None of that was going to happen to me!

And the best way to make sure of it was to stay awake! Then I wouldn't have the nightmares, and I'd be able to tell from one minute to the next if I was going blind or anything awful like that.

I took the sandwich out of the refrigerator, but I didn't want to stay in the apartment. I could see Paul's balcony, and even though I didn't see him anywhere, I still felt as if he was watching me.

I didn't like the idea that he could look in our windows, but closing the curtains at noon would give him the idea that I realized he spied on us. Suddenly it seemed important to me that I keep him from finding out anything I knew.

I had to get out of the apartment again, out into the sun, even though the light bothered me. It would be easier to forget my problems if I was outside.

I picked up the key and left. I'd eat while I walked around the neighborhood.

It was hot again. I walked south one block and then turned east, into a neighborhood I hadn't seen before. The houses were larger here, enclosed by fences and tall hedges. A small dog on a sun porch barked furiously at me. I hurried past and it stopped barking, then suddenly began again. I looked back.

A man wearing a hat and an overcoat was passing the house with the sun porch. He walked with his head down, hurrying.

An overcoat? He was wearing an overcoat in this weather?

Sneaking out, Kate? I'll find out where you're going. You can't trick me. I'll always find out.

I began running.

Chapter Five

The man didn't follow me. I'd run nearly two blocks before I dared to look back, and he wasn't there.

But I was afraid to slow down. When I saw the apartment house ahead, I took another look back and still didn't see the man in the overcoat.

Who was he? For a crazy moment, I wondered if it had been Paul. But it could have been any other man of his height and build.

I pulled open the door, ran down the hall, and started up the stairs. It was safe to slow down now. I was almost home.

I was halfway up the stairs when I thought I heard the dry rustle of wings above me. I looked up quickly, startled. The ceiling was bare.

But I'd *heard* birds fluttering there!

I began running again. The key. Which of my pockets held the key?

I reached the third floor and turned toward Shelly's apartment just as I found the key. My hand shook while I unlocked the deadbolt, and my heart pounded.

I opened the door and slammed it shut behind me. Only locking the deadbolt and fastening the chain didn't satisfy me—I wanted to block the door with something. Just as I decided to push Shelly's upholstered chair against the door, the phone rang.

The sound cut through the apartment like a scream. I held my breath, waiting for the second ring.

Who could it be? Shelly? Eloise? John D.?

The runner from my nightmares?

Paul?

I couldn't go on like this, panicking because of my bad dreams and imagined noises. My hand was trembling when I picked up the phone, but I convinced myself quickly that the worst thing that could happen to me was Shelly's finding out I'd left the apartment again without telling her.

"Is that you, Kate?"

Paul's voice stunned me. "What do you want?" I stammered.

"You're alone, aren't you?" he asked.

"No," I lied.

He laughed softly, "Liar, liar," he chanted. The line went dead.

I slammed down the phone and pressed my fingers to my lips. He sounded crazier than before.

I'd tell Shelly right away. She'd know what to do. I tried to call her, but I got a wrong number. I dialed again, and this time I got the company, but Shelly wasn't there.

I hung up without leaving a message. If she wasn't there, then she couldn't help me. Was he coming here? Should I leave the apartment?

I turned to look at the dining room window, opposite the apartment door. Paul wasn't on his balcony, but that didn't mean he wasn't watching from inside his apartment, maybe even with binoculars.

I hurried to the cord that closed the curtain and yanked it. It came loose in my hand.

I ran to my bedroom, tried to close that curtain, and fumbled desperately at it. It was stuck.

I ran into Shelly's room, where the window overlooked the roof of a large, old house. The cord on that curtain worked. Even though no one could see in Shelly's window, I closed the curtain.

Think! I told myself. I had to do something, tell someone, but my mind was blank. Maybe Shelly had returned to her office.

There was a phone extension in Shelly's room and I reached for it, then realized I couldn't remember the number.

The phone rang while my hand was over it.

Oh, no. Should I answer again?

I picked it up, but I was too frightened to speak. A woman on the phone said, "Mrs. Chamberlain? Is that you?"

It was a wrong number and I tried to speak, but my mouth was too dry.

"Oh, darn it anyway," the woman said, and she hung up.

My legs gave out and I sat down on the floor next to the bed. I couldn't think straight. What if Paul came here? I wondered. Could I keep him out?

I could call the police, but what would I say? Would they believe me, a stuttering kid? I'd only make myself sound like an idiot, accusing somebody I hardly knew of . . . of what? What had he done except make a weird phone call?

And follow me wearing an overcoat on a hot day, I thought. Hadn't it been him?

But what was the point of following me?

Unless he wanted a chance to hurt me.

Unless he really was the one who had hit me, and I'd actually become able to read his mind.

I didn't know what to do, and so I did nothing at all but sit there beside Shelly's bed, waiting. After a while my heart slowed down and beat normally.

The next time the phone rang, I picked it up quickly. I'd convinced myself that I could handle whatever came.

"How are you feeling, Kate?" my sister asked.

I could have cried because I was so relieved. "I'm okay," I said. "But Paul called here a while ago. I don't know what he wanted—he's really weird. But he scared me." I wanted to tell her that I thought he might have been following me, too, but I wasn't certain of that, and it was hard to believe.

"What did he say to you?" Shelly asked. She sounded angry.

"He asked me if I was alone," I said. "I said, 'No,' and he called me a liar. But it was as if he was teasing me and liked scaring me. Then he hung up. I think he watches everything that goes on here from his place. He knew I was alone."

"I'll handle him," Shelly said sharply. "He's a snoop. I've seen him standing on his balcony, openly watching me when I've been close to my windows or the lights are on. I keep the curtains closed a lot of the time when I'd like them open." She was silent for a moment, and then said, "I shouldn't have tolerated him. I can see now that I handled it wrong by ignoring him."

"What are you going to do?" I asked.

She laughed a little. "He's probably the world's biggest coward," she said. "People like that hate confrontation. So I'll confront him, as soon as we get home from the doctor's office this afternoon. I won't put up with him scaring you."

"You're not going to talk to him alone!" I protested.

"Not on your life," she said. She really laughed then. "I'll bring Eloise. She'll take on anybody."

She told me what time she'd pick me up to take me to the doctor, and when she hung up, I felt a lot better. It was obvious that my sister thought Paul was an irritating pest, but she wasn't afraid of him—so why should I be?

I got to my feet, feeling a little ashamed of myself. I'd had an accident which had scared me out of my wits. I'd been having nightmares and imagining some really weird things. It was true that Paul was repulsive. But I had enough common sense to see that there wasn't a connection between an ugly neighbor and my nightmares. It wouldn't be reasonable to believe that.

And nobody—except Molly—really believed that a person could read someone else's mind.

So when I walked out to the dining room on my way to the kitchen for a drink of water and saw Paul standing on his balcony, I ignored him.

He was gone when Shelly got home, but she climbed on a chair and yanked the curtain closed anyway.

"The cord broke once before," she said. "I'll fix it when I've got time, but for now, let's leave the curtain closed. I'm sick of Paul peering in here and treating us like fish in an aquarium."

She pulled off her jacket as she talked and tossed it over the back of a chair. "I called Eloise at the bookstore. She's going over to Paul's with me tonight—she wants the money he owes her. Afterward, we'll talk to John D.'s parents about Paul. We know they don't like him. Maybe they'll find a way to evict him if we complain enough."

Paul will blame me, I thought. He already hates me—just because I'm here. Was he jealous of me? It was a crazy idea, but then, Paul acted crazy.

I gave myself a mental shake to stop myself from following that line of thought. So he was crazy. That didn't mean he'd tried to hurt me.

But I'd read thrillers . . .

No, Kate! I told myself. Let it drop.

I didn't say anything more to my sister. I didn't want to sound as if I was making a fuss about Paul. If I worried Shelly much more, she'd call Dad, and then my parents would come home. I had to act my age, not like a scared little kid. Even Molly would probably handle this better than I.

I liked Shelly's doctor. Dr. Francis was small and plump, and she wore her hair in a long braid. She didn't look any older than Shelly, but she told me she had a daughter my age who was spending a month at summer camp.

She examined me and changed the bandage on my arm. "You've got a rotten headache, too, haven't you?" she asked. "I can tell by the way you're squinting."

"It hurts sometimes," I admitted.

"She's complained about it several times," Shelly added.

Dr. Francis pushed back my bangs and looked at the small, faint bruise, which had turned a little yellow by then. "Just because it doesn't look like much doesn't mean it doesn't hurt," she said. "But I haven't found any signs of concussion. I think you're lucky. Have you been sleeping well?"

"No," I said. "It's hard to get comfortable because I feel so stiff. And I have nightmares."

"Small wonder," the doctor said. "If you *didn't* have nightmares after being run down by a car I'd wonder about you. It'll take a while to get over being that scared. Don't blame yourself. You're entitled to be upset, especially since the police haven't caught the guy yet. It must make you mad."

"Yes," I said.

"Really mad," the doctor said.

"*Really* mad," I said.

She grinned. "You're entitled to that, too."

I grinned back at her.

"Shelly told me you didn't want your parents to know you've been hurt because they'll come home and their trip will be spoiled," the doctor said. "They're going to feel bad, no matter when they find out about it. Would you like me to call them and tell them you're doing fine?"

"If I'm fine, you don't need to call," I said.

She looked straight at me and finally smiled. "Okay. For now. But if the headaches don't go away in another day or so, I want to see you again, and then we'll have to talk to your parents."

I nodded. I wouldn't need to see her again. No one

53

had to tell my parents anything and interrupt the work that was so important to them.

We stopped on the way home for takeout food again. "You must think I've forgotten how to cook," Shelly told me as we drove home. "But this is easier."

"Especially since you and Eloise are going to see Paul," I said. The inside of the car smelled like barbecued ribs, and I was so hungry my mouth was watering.

Shelly laughed. "*Especially* since we're going over there. I hope you don't mind, but I told Eloise you'd watch Molly while we're taking on Paul. She's really not much bother."

I remembered how much I hated being in the apartment alone, so I said, "Molly's really cute. I'll be glad to watch her."

I'm really a mess, I thought, if a little kid can scare away the bogeyman for me.

Shelly and I ate off paper plates, and had just finished dinner when the doorbell rang. Once again I could hear Molly out in the hall, this time arguing about whether or not a quart of chocolate ice cream was enough for two people.

"But Kate will need more," she told her mother as Shelly let them in. "Anybody who's sick needs more ice cream."

Shelly took the ice cream Molly was carrying in one hand and stuck it in the freezer. The child held a videotape in the other, and she held that out to me.

"John D. hasn't been here with any of his tapes,

has he?'' she asked suspiciously. She was scowling a little. "We don't need any of his tapes. We don't need John D. here, either.''

"He's not coming,'' I said. "There'll just be the two of us.''

"And we'll only be gone a few minutes,'' Eloise said. "Molly, you're carrying on as if you'll be here for a week.''

"Put on the tape,'' Molly told me, ignoring her mother completely. "It's cartoons.''

I put on the tape. Molly and I were sitting side by side on the couch watching when Shelly and Eloise left.

"I'm looking forward to this,'' I heard Eloise say as Shelly closed the door.

"She gets madder than anybody else in Seattle,'' Molly said. "Mom, I mean, not Shelly. Mom can yell so loud you can hear her on the moon. Nobody ever yells back.'' Molly seemed quite proud of this.

I was relieved at Molly's news, because I'd been worrying about Shelly. She was so nice, so soft-spoken, that I wondered how she was going to handle Paul. Maybe she wouldn't have to. Eloise sounded as if she could take on an army.

"Oh, she can get mad, too,'' Molly said as she watched a cartoon dragon eating flowers.

"Who can?'' I asked, staring at her.

"Your sister.''

Molly had been reading my mind again. I didn't know whether to laugh or move a few inches away from her.

"What about you?'' I asked. "Do you get mad at Paul?''

She scowled. "I hate him."

She's afraid of him, I thought suddenly. He's done something to her. Scared her. Hurt her somehow.

She looked at me. "He's a bad man."

"What did he do?" I asked quietly.

She looked away and then back at me. "I think I forgot."

"Does your mother know?" I asked.

She hesitated a moment, and then blurted, "There was this old cat who lived behind the dumpster, and he kicked her and kicked her, and I told Mom and we went to find the cat but it was gone, and it never came back."

A cold shiver ran over me. I hated hearing about things like that. "I hope he moves away," I said.

"Me, too," Molly said. She sighed.

"Did something else happen?" I asked.

Molly looked up at me innocently. "No. Why?"

I shrugged. "You sorta look like you had something else to say."

"Not me," Molly said firmly. "That's all I've got to say."

I didn't know whether to believe her or not.

Shelly and Eloise were gone for nearly an hour and a half. When they returned, the cartoon tape was over and Molly and I were having our second helpings of chocolate ice cream.

"How did it go?" I asked. My stomach felt like the ice cream had turned to rocks.

Shelly looked furious. "The man is simply insane," she said. "He denied calling you, he denied watching us from his balcony, and he denied not paying Eloise for the books.''

I was so disappointed I couldn't think of anything to say. I suppose I'd been telling myself that Paul would apologize and promise never to bother us again.

"Then we went over to see John C. and his wife," Eloise said. "That turned out a little better. They won't renew his lease because the neighbors have complained so much about him. They wouldn't tell us what the complaints have been about, but they've already warned him that he has to move. Unfortunately, his lease isn't up until October.''

"He bangs on the walls and yells and screams in the middle of the night," Molly said. "He parks his car in other people's places. He steals other people's newspapers. He snoops in their garbage and even takes things out of the bins. That's what John D. told me.''

"Wonderful," Eloise said bitterly. "Well, I'm afraid we've done the best we can do for now. Paul's on notice that we'd better never see him looking in our direction again or we'll call the police . . .''

"He watches you, too?" I asked, amazed.

"Oh, sure," Eloise said. "Nobody on this side of our building has any privacy unless we close our curtains.''

It was awful, but I felt relieved to know that lots of other people were being bothered by Paul, too. I could relax. It wasn't just me.

Eloise and Molly went home then, and Shelly fixed iced tea for the two of us.

"I don't know if Eloise and I actually accomplished anything,'' Shelly said as she handed me my glass. ''Paul wouldn't let us in his apartment, but I got a quick peek past him. His bed is in the living room! When he noticed that I was trying to see inside, he came out in the hall with us and shut the door. I'll bet the rest of the place is empty. If he's rich, I don't know what he spends his money on.'' She sipped her tea before she went on. ''Well, medical school is expensive. Maybe that explains it.''

The apartment she described sounded like the one I'd seen in my mind. But that couldn't be! I must have caught a glimpse of it through his glass door without it really registering on me.

''What a day,'' Shelly said, holding the cold glass against her forehead. ''I've got a headache now, and I never get them, not unless I've bumped my head on something.''

''Tell me about it,'' I said. ''I never got headaches very often either, until now.''

''But I thought you were getting better,'' Shelly said. ''Oh dear. I upset you, didn't I? I shouldn't have ranted and raved about Paul so much.''

''My head's fine,'' I said. I took a deep swallow of my tea. ''Let's forget about Paul. We can leave the curtains closed and ignore him whenever we see him. I don't want to give him a chance to spoil my summer.''

''He won't,'' Shelly said. ''You're absolutely right. We've done everything we can, and we've got more important things to think about than that pathetic freak across the street.''

*　　*　　*

Afterward, a long time afterward, I wondered why it was so easy for me to convince myself that I had imagined almost everything. Was it because I'd always tried to avoid trouble of any kind? Because I was so shy? Or was it because I was stupid?

After I got ready for bed, I turned out the light in my bedroom and then, slowly, I opened my curtain. I wanted to see if there were lights on in Paul's apartment.

His curtains were open and all the lights were on. Now I could clearly see the room I had only seen in my imagination before—that bare room with almost nothing in it. I held my breath for a moment.

Paul wasn't there—at least, I didn't see him anywhere.

I closed the curtain, crawled into bed, and shut my eyes. I'll go to sleep and forget all about this, I told myself. It's only a coincidence.

Kate tattled on me, the rotten little sneak.

Well, she won't get away with it. I'll make her sorry she came here. I'll make them all sorry.

I was wide awake, not dreaming, and I could hear his voice. His thoughts.

He was thinking about me.

Chapter Six

I lay awake hour after hour, trying to forget that bare apartment across the street. After midnight, I got up and pulled back one side of the curtain to see if the lights were still on in Paul's apartment. They were out.

Maybe he was watching our building, standing there in the dark, thinking about us.

Planning something.

I dropped the corner of the curtain and scrambled into bed. My head ached again. For several minutes I tossed and turned, trying to get comfortable, trying to make myself think of something else—anything else!—instead of that apartment across the street.

Finally I got up and padded into the bathroom. Shelly must have aspirin in the medicine cabinet, I thought. I didn't care that the doctor didn't want me to take anything. I needed sleep, and I was exhausted from my headache.

I found a small bottle of headache pills that contained an aspirin substitute and shook two of them into my hand. As I filled a paper cup with water, Shelly knocked on the bathroom door. I gulped down the pills before I opened the door.

"Can't sleep again?" she asked. "Well, neither can

I. I keep going over and over in my mind how Paul acted when Eloise and I were there. He actually implied that you've been spying on him ever since you got here. I can't remember ever being that angry at anyone before. I wanted to knock him down and jump up and down on him.''

"I know what you mean," I said. "Don't forget I was the one he phoned and called a liar. Jumping up and down on him is good. I can go along with that." I was desperate to cheer us up, but my feeble attempt at humor didn't work.

"If I catch him watching us once more, I'll call the police," Shelly said.

"Do you think it would do any good?" I asked, suddenly bitter. "Probably he'd say it's his right to look anywhere he wants."

"I suppose," Shelly said. "But Eloise says that if enough of us call and complain, maybe they'd have to warn him, at least."

While she talked, I ran cold water on a washcloth, wrung it out, and pressed it against my forehead. My frustration with Paul and my anger about the accident weren't helping my head.

And now I was feeling the way I did the previous spring, when Bernina and her rotten friends turned my life into a nightmare!

"Hey, what's up?" Shelly asked. "You look as though you just tasted poison."

I tried to laugh but it came out more like a croak. "You aren't far off. This whole mess with Paul reminds me of last spring, when I finally got up enough courage to complain to the guidance counselor at school about the kids in the first-floor locker room who teased me all the time because I stutter," I said.

"Oh, honey," Shelly said sadly. "That's awful. What happened?"

"They all denied it, of course, and Bernie—she's the ring-leader—Bernie said they went out of their way to be nice to me, even though I'd stolen things from all of them and acted crazy most of the time."

Talking about it made my throat tighten up, as if I had a big lump in it. My stuttering got worse, too. I saw myself in the bathroom mirror, all pale and teary-eyed, and I wanted to slap myself silly so I'd shape up.

Shelly stared at me. "What happened?"

"The counselor told me I ought to be grateful I had such good friends instead of trying to make trouble for them," I said. I could hardly talk now because of the lump in my throat. "Then she gave me a new locker in the basement, all by myself in a section no one uses. 'Because you can't get along with anybody,' she said. It was so far away from the side of the school where the busses stop that I didn't have time to get anything out of it after my last class. I had to carry everything around with me all afternoon or end up walking home. Anne—she's my best pal—finally asked me to share her locker on the second floor by the stairs. Bernie found out and tattled, and then Anne ended up with a locker so far away that she had to carry her stuff around, too. At least she didn't get mad at me."

"What did Dad do?" Shelly asked.

"I didn't tell him or Mom for a long time," I said. "It sounded so dumb. And I was afraid of what the counselor might say. She wasn't very nice. And I sure didn't want to go back to the speech therapist again, because it didn't do that much good before. Anyway, I figured that I already had enough trouble. All I wanted to do was survive junior high.''

"I remember feeling like that," Shelly said. "So when did Dad and your mom find out?''

I pressed the damp cloth to my mouth for a moment. I wasn't certain I should tell. But she was my sister, and she'd always been wonderful to me.

"One Sunday night I got to thinking about going back to school the next morning, and I started crying and couldn't stop. They wanted to know what was wrong, so I told them. Both of them went to school the next day to talk to the principal, but it didn't help. He only sent them to the counselor, who told them I was too high-strung and had trouble remembering which things belonged to me and which things belonged to other people. Nothing my family tried to do helped. Pretty soon all the kids in school knew about it. Things got worse than they had been to start with.''

Shelly shook her head slowly. "That's really terrible. I didn't have that hard a time in junior high, but I can remember thinking I probably wouldn't live through it.''

I took the cloth off my forehead and stared at her. "You?" I asked. "Everybody was always crazy about you. You were always gorgeous, and you didn't stutter or say stupid things . . .''

"Oh, listen to her," Shelly said, laughing. "Maybe I didn't have a problem with my speech, but I talked too much and one girl called me 'motor mouth' in art class and I cried for weeks about it. I never wanted to go back—and it was my favorite class! But I was sure I was ugly because I was taller than anybody else, and my ears stuck straight out, and my feet were huge.''

''Look at you now,'' I said. ''I bet you don't worry about anything like that anymore.''

''Are you serious?'' Shelly asked, laughing again. ''I don't think anybody is ever satisfied with the way she looks. But right now I'm worrying about whether you're getting enough sleep—and if you'll ever be allowed to stay with me again since I've done such a rotten job of taking care of you.''

To my astonishment, she began crying.

''What happened was my fault!'' I said. ''You didn't have anything to do with somebody hitting me with a car. And as for Paul, well, anybody can have a crazy neighbor. Anne's family moved to a different house six blocks away because their next-door neighbor wouldn't leave them alone. Paul will move out in October, and then everything will be fine.''

''But you won't be here to enjoy it,'' Shelly said. She wiped her eyes with a handful of tissues. ''Come on, sis, let's knock this off and go to bed. One way or another I'll make Paul leave us alone so you don't have to worry about him. And one way or another the police will find out who hit you.''

''If you say it, I'll do my best to believe it,'' I said.

I felt so good about our talk that I was certain everything would turn out right. Why didn't I tell her how I had begun hearing Paul's thoughts sometimes? Why didn't I tell her that I knew what his room looked like?

Why didn't I tell her about the dream runner?

I went back to bed and wondered who he was. Was

he Paul? Or was he the man who hit me?

Or were they all the same?

It was all coincidence! I had to believe that or I'd scare myself to death.

But if I really believed it was nothing but a stupid coincidence, why didn't I tell Shelly?

We needed a good laugh, my sister and I. But I didn't know where we could find one.

Rain began falling at dawn, pattering against the window. I lay awake listening, soothed by the sound, and gradually I drifted into that half-sleep state where nothing seems quite real, but nothing is exactly a dream, either.

In my mind, I floated freely inside the bare room across the street, as light as a wisp of fog. I saw someone lying in a bed, but I couldn't tell who it was. I saw a newspaper in a chair and a TV in a corner on the floor.

I saw photos of my sister on the walls.

Some of them were very good, but some were blurred. She never appeared to have been aware of the camera. Here was one of her getting into her car. Here was one taken as she walked down a street somewhere. She was wearing a pink raincoat. There were several of her with Eloise, and one showing her sharing an ice-cream cone with Molly.

I drifted on, and looked at an untidy heap of papers on the small table, but I didn't bother reading them. I passed by the kitchen, and saw dirty dishes on the counter, an empty liquor bottle, and several plastic bottles that contained pills and tablets.

I turned into a hall, went around a corner and saw

what seemed to be a bedroom, but it contained only a few open cardboard boxes filled with jumbled clothes and some cooking utensils. From the appearance of the room, a person could have moved into the apartment the day before.

I glided back to the living room where the person still slept. I saw the binoculars on the floor under the window. In my dream state, I wasn't shocked—or even worried. I only observed, like a camera.

But then the occupant of the bed stirred and sat up. Paul.

He looked around the room as if he sensed my presence. I withdrew to the kitchen, still unconcerned.

"Who's here?" he asked harshly. "I know someone's here."

I froze in sudden fright. The part of my mind that was in the room was unable to speak.

"Who's here?" he yelled. He jumped out of bed and swung around, like a boxer looking for someone to punch.

I shrank back, afraid he might find me. I wanted to stop this, stop watching, stop *being there*. But I didn't know how to control the part of my mind that had sent me there.

"I know someone's watching me," Paul said. He pivoted slowly and stared straight at me. His tan eyes bulged for a moment, but then he smiled.

He could see me!

"Kate?" he asked. "Is it you, little Kate?"

He moved toward me deliberately. "I don't like this," he said softly, shaking his head. "No, no. I won't put up with anybody spying on me. Get away from me or I'll make you sorry, more sorry than you've ever been or ever dreamed of being. You've turned Shelly against me and now she's plotting something. This is your fault. Get out!''

I wanted to leave, but I didn't know how. I wished and prayed and begged to go home to Shelly's apartment and my bed there, but part of my mind, the conscious part, was in Paul's apartment, cowering in his kitchen as he came closer and closer.

''Don't make me hurt you again, Kate,'' he said. ''Don't make me do it.''

I was helpless.

He lunged at me.

Light exploded and I hurtled into bits. Birds wheeled around me, shrieking in terror. I was sucked into darkness, and then into the rainy dawn.

I was back in my own bed, sitting up, hands clapped over my mouth so I wouldn't scream.

He knew! He knew I'd been thinking about him, that I had somehow traveled to his apartment, and had watched him.

And he *was* the one who had hit me!

After a long moment, I got up and pulled back the curtain. My heart beat so hard I wondered if Shelly could hear it down the hall in her bedroom.

Across the street, Paul stood in his window watching me. He was too far away for me to see his expression, but I knew he was laughing.

I got up when Shelly's alarm went off. While she was in the shower, I set the table for breakfast and poured orange juice into our glasses. The curtain by the table was closed. Shelly hadn't fixed the cord yet, but I didn't care if she never did. I didn't want to look across the street while I ate.

Shelly seemed tired when she came out for breakfast. I felt responsible—she'd sleep better if it wasn't for me.

"I need a cup of coffee," she said after she finished her cereal. "I've only got time for instant, though." She pushed back her chair and carried her bowl and glass to the kitchen. "Heavens, it's still raining," she said as she looked out the window over the sink. "I hate to drive in heavy traffic when it's raining this hard, so I'll leave a little early and catch the bus."

"It was so hot yesterday that I didn't expect rain," I said.

Tell her about last night! I told myself. Tell her that you know Paul is the one who hit you.

No, no, she'd think you're crazy. She'd call Dad right away, and his and Mom's summer would be ruined.

Crybaby Kate, making trouble again.

"I always expect rain here," she said. "But I don't mind it anymore." She heated a cup of water in the microwave and stirred instant coffee into it. "How are you feeling this morning? How's your head?"

"Better," I said, remembering the pills I shouldn't have taken. They had helped. I'd take more if the headache came back.

"As soon as I finish my coffee, I'll change the bandage for you," Shelly said.

"I can probably leave it off now," I said.

"We'll see how it looks," she said. She seemed distracted. Maybe it was only because she was tired.

"Is everything all right?" I asked.

Shelly sighed. "I had nightmares myself last night," she said.

"What about?" I asked without thinking. What if she asked me about mine? This was no time to exchange stories about bad dreams. My story could ruin the summer.

She shrugged. "I can't really remember what it was about. I suppose I had a bad night because Eloise and I argued with Paul. It was so frustrating! Darn that rotten snoop."

"Keep away from him after this," I said. "Even if he tries to talk to you, don't answer."

"You're right. If he calls here, hang up. We'll simply cut him out of our lives, and maybe he'll take the hint."

Oh, no he won't, I thought. Paul will never take a hint.

We decided I didn't need a bandage on my arm any longer. The scrape was healing and had scabbed over——not a pretty sight, of course, but it looked better than it had. I'd wear long-sleeved shirts for a few days.

Shelly went to her room to finish dressing, and came out wearing a pink raincoat.

The sight of it startled me. It was the same coat I'd seen her wearing in the photo on Paul's wall.

"What's wrong?" Shelly asked when she saw me looking at her. "Don't you like the coat?"

"It's great," I said. My lips were numb with shock. "I love the color."

She looked down at it and smiled. "So do I. I bought it in Chicago when I was there on business. I thought I had the only one around here, but a few weeks ago I saw a woman with one exactly like it in the grocery store.'' She pulled the hood over her head and started for the door. ''I'll call you during the day,'' she said. ''Don't go anywhere without telling me first, okay?''

''I'm going to catch up on my reading,'' I said.

But as it turned out, I didn't have time to even open a book. After I showered and finished dressing, Eloise called to ask if I wanted to go clothes shopping with her and Molly.

''I've got the day off and I'd appreciate some grown-up company,'' she said.

I wanted to get out of the apartment house, but I knew I had to keep my promise to Shelly. ''I'd love to go,'' I said. ''But I need to get in touch with Shelly first so she knows where I'm going.''

Eloise said she'd stop by in half an hour, so I called Shelly right away. I was surprised to catch her at her desk. She thought the shopping trip was a good idea, and asked me if I had enough money.

''Mom gave me all I'll need,'' I said.

After she hung up, I grabbed my Windbreaker and waited for Eloise. I'd be glad to get out of there, for as long as possible. Shelly's apartment was pretty, and the building was very nice, in its old-fashioned way. But there was still something about it that made me feel uncomfortable. Maybe it was the high ceilings and tall, narrow windows that made it seem mysterious and a little sinister.

The building that Paul lived in was modern and looked quite cheerful. That was the place that ought to seem spooky, I thought. But from the appearance of the building, you'd never guess that somebody that crazy lived there.

Eloise, Molly, and I shopped for clothes in a mall in the suburbs, had lunch in a restaurant overlooking Puget Sound, and, standing outside in the rain, fed sea gulls with our leftover french fries. My sister's neighbors were good company. I felt better than I had for days.

By the time we got home, the rain had stopped. We found John D. vacuuming the carpet in the back hall, and Molly greeted him by accusing him of failing to return one of her favorite tapes to the rental store.

"Mom called them to reserve it again, but they said somebody didn't bring it back," Molly declared. "I know it was you."

"I bet it's only kid stuff," John D. told her in a patronizing voice. "I don't watch tapes like that. Hi, Kate. What's in all those shopping bags?"

He had such a great smile that it took me two tries to get out the words, "New clothes."

"Great," he said. If he'd noticed how much I stuttered, he didn't let on. "Put on something new and let's go find something to do."

"I think you've already got something to do, John D.," Eloise said. She pointed at the vacuum cleaner. "Besides, Kate's probably tired. I don't think Shelly would like it if we wore her out."

John D. looked offended. "I'm practically done here," he said. "And I wasn't going to run Kate up and down a mountain. I just thought she might like to check out a few things in the neighborhood."

I called Shelly again, and she said it was all right for me to spend part of the afternoon with John D., as long as I promised to go home if I felt tired.

"I can go, too," Molly announced after I hung up.

"When pigs fly," John D. said.

Molly left under protest, dragged off by her mother, who apologized as she went.

John D. and I agreed to meet fifteen minutes later by the front door. That gave me time to change into a new shirt and jeans and brush my hair. I was in and out of the apartment so fast that I didn't have time to worry about being alone.

Still, when I hurried down the stairs, I heard that strange, dry rustling sound overhead again, and I looked up quickly, still expecting to see a bird trapped inside the building. Nothing was there.

My headache began abruptly.

I didn't go back for more headache pills, but ran down to meet John D., who was leaning against the wall by the door.

"Let's not go out this door," he said as soon as he saw me.

"Why?" I asked.

"That jerk across the street is hanging around."

I moved to look out the glass panel in the door, but John D. blocked my path. "You can't see him from here," he said. "Anyway, the front door will save time."

I didn't ask why John D. didn't want Paul to see us. I didn't want to know. Every new thing I learned about that man only scared me more.

"Do you work in this building every day?" I asked, to move the subject as far away from Paul as I could.

John D. held the other door open for me and followed me out. "No, it just feels that way. My parents think stuff up for me to do so I won't get into trouble with all this vacation time on my hands. You know, I could be robbing banks, high-jacking Metro busses. Mostly, around here, I get in the custodian's way, but it keeps my parents happy."

"What do you do the rest of the time?" I asked. We walked down a narrow street under trees that still dripped from the rainfall earlier. Overhead, though, I saw blue patches in the sky.

"You name it," he said cheerfully. "We've got a lot of good beaches and some great places to bike. I like tennis, too. How about you?"

I heard him, but my headache got worse suddenly, and I had trouble thinking straight. DRUM DRUM DRUM.

"Hey, you okay?" John D. asked.

"Sure," I lied. "Where are we going?"

"A friend of mine lives on the next block, and her poodle had puppies last week. They're really cute, and I thought you'd like to see them."

DRUM DRUM DRUM.

Where do you think you're going, Kate?

I gasped and clutched John D.'s arm.

"What's wrong?" he asked. "You look sick. Maybe we should go back."

"Don't turn around," I babbled. "Don't look back. Just keep walking."

He began turning, to look behind, but I cried, "No, please! Don't look."

We walked a little faster. "Is somebody following us?" he asked. "Is that what's wrong?"

The drumming in my head almost drowned him

out. I was so scared I was ready to cry. "I don't know," I said. "Just keep walking. Is your friend's house close by? Can we hurry?"

DRUM DRUM DRUM. *You can't stay here. I don't want you here. Don't make me hurt you.*

John D. steered me around a corner. "There's the house, that tan one with the big deck," he said.

The pounding in my head quieted suddenly, and instead I heard the steady, soft padding of a runner's feet. The person didn't follow us, but crossed the street behind us. A passing car drowned out the sound.

I didn't look back.

"I want to go home," I said suddenly. "You're right. I feel sick." It wasn't exactly true, but I needed to go home and lock the door. And maybe even crawl under the bed.

"But we're almost there," he said.

"Maybe I can see the puppies some other time," I said. "I need to go home."

"Let's go, then," John D. said. He didn't sound angry. He sounded worried. "Can't you tell me what was wrong back there?"

How could I explain? What would he think of me if I told him I'd heard a voice in my mind and it scared me, because I believed it was Paul.

"My head began aching again," I said. We turned the corner and started back where we'd come from.

I took a quick look in the direction where the running footsteps had gone. Far down the block I saw a runner in white shorts and a white shirt, elbowing his way between a couple.

John D. looked in the same direction. "Jeez, it's Paul," he said. "I wish he had a different hobby.

Somebody ought to broadcast a bulletin warning everybody to stay off the streets every time he's out running. He practically kills people.''

He looked over at me then. ''You knew he was behind us, right? Did he scare you?''

''Yes,'' I admitted.

''He's nuts, you know,'' John D. said. ''I mean *really* nuts. He tells everybody he's a medical student, but there isn't a single book in his apartment. Don't medical students have to do a lot of reading? He doesn't own a book, not even a paperback mystery.''

I stared at John D. He was right. I hadn't seen any books there when I—or that floating part of my mind—had drifted around inside the apartment. But how did John D. know?

''You've been in his apartment?'' I asked.

''Too many times,'' he grumbled. ''A few months ago, every time I'd be over there vacuuming and he saw me, he'd think up something for me to do. 'Take these packages up to my apartment.' 'I can't get one of the windows open.' 'The door sticks.' ''

''And he lets you inside?'' I asked, wondering if he'd seen the photos of my sister.

''Yeah,'' John D. said. He ducked under a low-hanging branch. ''Well, he used to let me inside. He quit asking me to do stuff after a while. Now he's always accusing me of getting into his place when he's not home and snooping through his things. The place is practically empty, and, as far as I could see, he hasn't got anything a burglar would think was worth stealing. He's nuts.''

''Yes,'' I said. ''He is.'' The day was warm, and yet I shivered.

A car came down the street too fast and I flinched when it passed us. It reminded me of being hit.

I wondered what kind of car Paul had. And if it showed any signs of having hit a bike.

"Okay, here's home," John D. said. "I'll go up the stairs with you. Maybe you'd better call your sister and tell her you're not feeling so hot."

"I'm better now," I said. "I guess I was just tired."

We climbed the steps side by side, and John D. talked about the puppies I didn't get a chance to see.

I didn't hear the sound of wings that time.

John D. left me at my door. I unlocked it and went straight to my bedroom. It was hot and stuffy, but I didn't want to open the window in case Paul had returned home and was watching.

Suddenly I lost my temper. Why should I try to rest in a room that was this hot and miserable? I opened the window and stared defiantly across the street. I didn't see anyone.

But then the phone began to ring.

I knew it wasn't Shelly. I don't know how, but I was certain. I lay down on my bed and gritted my teeth and waited.

The phone rang ten times while my head ached and my room filled with the sounds of wildly beating wings. Then the answering machine clicked on.

I know you're there I know you're there I know you're there.

The man's voice boomed in my mind, not on the machine. I couldn't escape it.

I got up to check the machine. The call counter said zero—he had hung up without speaking.

He liked frightening me. He wanted to drive me out of Shelly's apartment. He had tried to hurt me. Maybe he even wanted to kill me. But who would believe me? If I said one word of this to Shelly, she'd have to call Dad. I know I would, if she'd been the one who was hit by a car—and was now having hallucinations.

I had to find a way to help myself.

I shut my eyes and took a deep breath. Do you hear me, Paul? I asked him in my mind. Do you know I'm thinking about you?

Stop it stop it stop it!

I was startled by the hysteria in his voice. I'd gotten through to him that easily?

You leave me alone! Get out of here! Stop spying on me!

He thought I was drifting around in his apartment again. He didn't know where I was this time.

Why not?

What are you trying to do? his mind shouted into my mind.

I would not answer. I tried to imagine a thick wall around me, too thick for his thoughts to penetrate.

Where are you? His voice was fainter now. *Kate! I'm warning you! Don't play games with me!*

I made my imaginary wall even thicker.

I'll find you . . . I could barely hear him now.

I doubled the thickness of the wall.

Silence.

I had learned something.

Chapter Seven

I had a grip on my nerves by the time Shelly got home, and it was a good thing too, because she wasn't alone. Andy was with her, and they were excited about picnic plans.

"The weather's cleared up," Andy said. "It's a shame to waste an afternoon like this, so we thought we'd take you to Green Lake for a picnic. How does that sound?"

"Great," I said, even though that wasn't how I felt. But I could tell from their expressions that they loved the idea.

"We know a great place where we can buy everything we need," Shelly said. "You'll love the food."

I couldn't help but laugh. "You did forget how to cook, didn't you?" I said.

She stripped off her pink raincoat and threw it over the back of a chair. "No, but we need to do some celebrating because you're here, and so far we haven't done much. Are you feeling up to it? John D. didn't tire you out, did he?"

"Did you see him downstairs?" I asked quickly. I didn't want him telling her anything about that afternoon.

"Heavens, no," she said, laughing. "John D.

doesn't work long hours. Are you tired? Did he run your legs off?''

"No," I said. "I love picnics. Are we leaving now?"

"We'll give the commuter traffic a chance to cool off," Andy said. He looked around, puzzled. "Hey, Kate, have you been sitting here with the curtains closed? You still have a headache, don't you?"

"It's not bad, honestly," I said. I looked at Shelly, waiting for her to answer about the curtains. Did she want Andy to know about Paul?

"We broke the cord that opens and closes those curtains, and I haven't had time to fix it yet," Shelly said smoothly. "Sit down, Andy, and entertain Kate while I change clothes."

Andy sat on the other end of the couch. "You like school?" he asked me.

Grown-ups always ask kids if they like school, but he didn't need to know the horrible truth. "Sure," I said. "I like school most of the time, anyway. But by the end of August, I always miss it and I start looking forward to going back."

He laughed and said, "I remember feeling like that. Shelly says you're smart."

It was my turn to laugh. "I pass everything, if that's what you mean. I wish I were an artist like Shelly, though." I turned and pointed at the beautiful pencil drawing of deer on the wall behind us. "I wish I could do something like that."

"I imagine she practiced a lot before she got that good," he said. "If you practiced, maybe you could do the same thing."

"I don't think so. Shelly's something special."

"That's the truth," he said, and he smiled.

He was really nice, and I was glad he liked my sister. He was completely different from Paul, who apparently had once thought he'd had a chance with Shelly. He had to be crazy if he actually believed someone like my sister could ever have cared for somebody like him. She'd made a big enough mistake feeling sorry for Paul. Look what that had got her!

I had to stop myself from thinking about that horrible man. I didn't know what to do about what was happening to me, and, until I had a plan, I had to keep my mouth shut or end up having everybody think I'd gone crazy or had brain damage.

And I had to stop finding spooky, mysterious things everywhere. It would only make everything worse, and even more confusing.

We bought everything we needed for our picnic at a small, crowded deli a few blocks away, and then drove to the lake. We were lucky—there was one table left near the parking lot, and from it we had a good view of the lake.

"I'm starved," I said as I helped Shelly and Andy set the table.

"Good," Shelly said. "That means you're getting better. How was that headache today?"

"It didn't bother me much," I lied. "In fact, it doesn't hurt at all right now." That last part was the truth anyway.

We didn't talk much as we finished all the salad and fried chicken. It wasn't until Shelly passed a plastic bowl of fruit over that I said, "I don't think I'll need to eat again for the rest of the month."

"Oh, yes you will," Shelly said. "You look as if you've lost weight since you got here, and we can't have that."

"Does anybody want to go for a walk?" Andy asked. "A short one would do us good."

"I will if Kate will," Shelly said.

"I'd rather sit here and watch everybody else walk," I said.

"Good for you," Shelly said. "I was hoping somebody else felt as lazy as I do."

She began clearing off the table, and Andy turned sideways on his bench to watch the bikers on the path whiz by. I looked past him, watching a group of kids talking and laughing. They were close to my age, and reminded me of John D., as well as Anne and a few other friends back home, kids I'd be seeing again when summer was over.

Kids I was beginning to wish I hadn't left behind! Rotten Bernie was there, too, but I didn't see much of her during school breaks. I could have had a nice summer at home, if my parents hadn't gone on that trip.

And then I saw that someone was standing in the shadow of an evergreen tree, a thin figure dressed in dark sweats.

DRUM DRUM DRUM DRUM.

Suddenly my head ached horribly. The evening light seemed blinding. My eyes watered and stung.

I see you, Shelly. I see him, too. I know what you're doing. You're not going to get away with dumping me. I'll make you sorry, you and that brat of a sister.

I tried to get to my feet, but my legs seemed to have turned to rubber.

I gave you a chance, Shelly. A better chance than you deserved. I thought you were different, but you weren't. You're no better than the others. And you brought that girl here and now you've taken up with HIM.

Go away, I thought as hard as I could. Get away from us.

You tried to put the girl between us so I wouldn't notice when you began sneaking around with that guy . . .

Leave us alone! I thought wildly. Go away!

You betrayed me, Shelly. You aren't worthy . . . aren't worthy . . . aren't worthy . . .

I was too panicky to remember at first about the wall I'd put up before. When I remembered it, my head hurt so much I was ready to cry. I concentrated as hard as I could, built the wall foot by foot, and thought over and over, GET AWAY!

You'll be sorry, Shelly. I'll fix you . . .

His thoughts were fading away. In my mind, I built the wall higher and higher, until it reached the sky. I made it thicker, until it covered everything. GET AWAY! I yelled in my mind.

Silence. The figure was gone.

"Kate, what's wrong?" Shelly asked.

I blinked. "What?"

"You look as if your head is hurting again."

"It is, a little," I said. I rubbed my temples. "It's not too bad, though."

"Time to go home," Andy said. "The wind's picking up, anyway, and it'll be cold here pretty soon."

I followed them back to Andy's car, looking all

around the parking lot to see if Paul was nearby. But I didn't see him.

Of course, I didn't know what his car looked like. Maybe I should find out.

Soon.

If it had a dent on it that looked as though it could have come from hitting a bike, then I'd know for sure that Paul was the runner in my dreams. Then I'd know for sure how far he was willing to go to get rid of me.

But then what would I do?

When we got home, I told Shelly I thought I'd go straight to bed. I admitted only to being tired and added that all that fresh air had made me sleepy. Actually, my head still ached, too. I wanted nothing more than a long sleep without dreams interrupting it.

The room had held in the heat and it was stuffy, too, so I peeked cautiously through my window to see if Paul was outside on his balcony. He wasn't anywhere in sight, so I opened the curtain and the window to let in the cool, fresh evening air.

But I didn't turn on my light, just in case he was watching from inside his apartment. I undressed hurriedly in the dark.

Then suddenly I was overwhelmed with resentment. This was all so stupid! Here I was, cringing inside a room, afraid to turn on my light because a Peeping Tom lived across the street and I was afraid of him.

But why shouldn't I be afraid? He was dangerous. Wasn't he?

I was sorry I'd eaten so much at the picnic, because

I felt sick. I stretched out on my bed and closed my eyes.

My imagination was only adding to my problems. I'd been hit by a car and I was lucky to be alive. Coincidentally, Shelly had a crazy neighbor who had a crush on her and pestered her. There couldn't be any connection between those two things.

There better not be! Because if Shelly was in any sort of danger, I had to do the right thing and get in touch with Dad.

And just what would Shelly think if I said we had to call Dad because she was in danger from Paul? She'd really think I was crazy then, because news like that would put my parents on the next plane. She didn't want that any more than I did.

I turned over on my side and tried to get comfortable. I could hear Shelly and Andy talking in the living room. The faint neighborhood noises I could hear through the window sounded friendly, not threatening.

Had Paul followed us to Green Lake? I'd thought so, but now I was beginning to wonder. My imagination, never exactly dormant, might have conjured everything up.

Everything, including the voice in my mind and the drifting visits to Paul's apartment, seemed too fantastic to be true. And I had headaches because I'd hit my head.

Maybe Mom was right—I read too many thrillers. Sometimes I read books that scared me silly.

And then I remembered that awful incident with the kids who teased me because I stuttered. The school counselor hadn't believed me. She'd said I was exaggerating, maybe even imagining things. I'd never been so humiliated, and I never wanted to feel that way again. Never.

At this point, I was more than willing to believe I'd read too many scary books. All I wanted was peace and quiet.

Peace and quiet and a good summer with Shelly.

Peace . . .

He was in bed, staring without blinking at his ceiling light. He didn't know I was there again, drifting above him, watching him.

She's learning too much, that Kate, that stupid, stuttering little brat. She's thinking too much. She's wondering about me. Maybe she's asking questions. Who could tell her something about me? John D. might. And that little red-haired monster. What's her name? Molly! But what do they really know?

All of this is Shelly's fault. She put me in danger by bringing Kate here, and she knows it. She's ruined everything. How does she expect me to go on caring about her when she tricks me?

I'll have to do something.

That Kate—she could have powers. She could have the powers I need! She comes here whenever she wants. She snoops. Maybe she tells.

I've got to get rid of both of them now. I made a mistake thinking that Shelly was the one I've promised myself. The promised one would never treat me this way, sneaking around behind my back, bringing a stranger here to block my path . . .

The one I promised myself would never betray me with another man!

He sat up suddenly and stared around. "Kate?" he

asked. His face contorted. "IT'S YOU! I KNOW YOU'RE HERE!"

He was yelling at the top of his lungs, and someone in the apartment below him began pounding and yelling, "Quiet up there! You shut up, you moron!"

But Paul didn't notice anything but me. He had located me, and his tan eyes bulged. "There you are! he screamed, and he leaped up from his mattress. "I can feel you're there, watching me, spying on me! I can feel you!"

"Shut up, you maniac, or we'll call the cops!" the voice downstairs bellowed. More pounding followed. "We'll really do it this time!"

I tried to force myself out of Paul's apartment and back into my own room, but I hung there, suspended over his head, completely helpless and wild with fright. The wall! I had to build it quickly! But I didn't seem to know how to do it anymore.

"Get out of here, or I'll kill you!" Paul screamed.

"Shut up!" the man downstairs yelled.

Paul's attention switched away from me. He stamped on the floor. "*You* shut up, you filthy swine!" he screamed at the man below him.

Go, get out of here, I told myself. I concentrated on the curtain over the window that faced the street and tried to imagine myself plunging through it as fast as lightning, as if it was nothing more than a veil of mist.

Light exploded around and through me.

I found myself sitting up in bed, shaking with fright.

It took a few minutes before my heart stopped hammering against my ribs. I'd had a terrible nightmare, but everybody knows nightmares can't hurt anybody.

I reached out to turn on the bedside lamp, but then I remembered that the curtain was still open, so I crawled out of bed and hurried over to close it.

The lights in Paul's apartment were on, but his curtains were closed and I couldn't see anything.

From below, in the street, I could hear a faint scraping. I leaned out the open window and saw nothing. The sound had seemed to come from directly below the window, but the broad stone ledge under the window was in the way. If something—or someone—was there, I couldn't see.

Then suddenly a white cat ran out and disappeared behind a car parked at the curb. I took a deep breath and almost laughed aloud as I closed the window and the curtain. A cat. That ought to be a lesson to me, I thought.

I had to concentrate on something besides Paul. I turned on the bedside light and picked up the book I'd begun reading on the plane. Okay, it was a thriller. But it was fiction, a made-up story.

And my visits to Paul's apartment weren't any more real than the book. I had to believe that, because *nobody* else would take my story seriously.

My story.

I closed my eyes and thought, Oh, please, don't let me be crazy. All this bad stuff comes from having such terrible headaches. And maybe even jet lag.

Although who ever heard of anybody getting jet lag without crossing a time zone?

I blinked hard and looked down at the book.

Gonna get you, Kate.

I blinked again and read the first line on the page.

Gonna get you, Kate. Gonna fix you.

I threw the book away from me in horror and it hit the wall.

I was crazy. I was certain of it now.

Chapter Eight

I didn't get much sleep, and when I did doze off, I had brief, scrambled dreams I couldn't seem to remember in the morning. It wasn't my worst night since I arrived in Seattle, but I woke up tired again.

A hard rain began falling a few minutes before Shelly left for her office.

"I should take the car today," she said. "I need to stop at the grocery store on the way home from work. But I hate driving in weather like this."

"Leave me a list and I'll go to the store for you," I said as I spread strawberry jam on my toast. "I don't mind walking in the rain."

And, I added silently to myself, it'll be a chance to get out of this depressing apartment.

Every day the place bothered me a little more than it had the day before. It was as if my nightmares had taken on some sort of strange existence of their own. There was a kind of electricity that crackled in the air around me, waiting for me to drop my guard.

"Are you sure you're up to it?" Shelly asked. She had slipped on the pink raincoat again and was buttoning it while she talked.

"Positive. But I could ask John D. if he'll come

with me, if that would make you feel better.''

Shelly grinned. ''He's awfully cute, isn't he? Everybody likes him. His phone number's in the little red address book on my desk, listed under his father, John C. Have you ever asked him about their names?''

''I've thought about it,'' I said. ''But I've got a hunch there's a really dumb reason.''

''So do I.'' Shelly grinned as she wrote out a grocery list. ''Here you go. Add anything you like.'' She dug through her purse until she found her wallet, and then handed me several ten dollar bills. ''If there's anything left, treat yourself and John D. to a snack.''

As soon as she closed the door behind her, I gathered up our breakfast dishes and took them to the kitchen. When I looked out the window over the sink, I caught a glimpse of Shelly's wind-blown pink raincoat as she crossed the intersection and headed for the bus stop.

A man in a raincoat and hat walked on the opposite sidewalk, and when Shelly disappeared, he hurried across the street and turned the same corner.

Was it Paul? I couldn't tell because he'd kept his head down, but it wouldn't have surprised me that he'd actually follow Shelly to the bus stop. When she used her car, did he follow in his? That wouldn't have surprised me, either.

I glanced toward Paul's apartment, and saw nothing moving but the driving rain that gushed down.

Last night seemed a million light-years away. I was doing myself a lot of damage with my fears and nightmares. And the things that popped into my mind during daylight hours were putting me under a lot of stress, too. What was true and what wasn't? I had no idea.

All I knew for certain was that I hated staying in this old building alone.

As soon as I dressed, I called John D.'s house. Luckily, he answered the phone himself, thank goodness, so I didn't have to go through a stuttering conversation with either of his parents.

"You want to go to the grocery store with me this morning?" I asked.

"Did you read my mind or what?" he asked.

Goosebumps raised on my arms.

"I was trying to think up a way of getting out of sweeping the laundry room across the street from your place, and you just handed it to me. Hold on a second while I tell my dad that you need me to help you. He knows all about you and he'll understand it's my civic duty to carry your grocery bags home for you."

John D. dropped his phone noisily on something hard, practically breaking my eardrum. While I waited, I tucked the phone between my ear and shoulder and tried to rub the goosebumps away from my arms. Even the most innocent mention of mind reading made me nervous those days.

John D. was back. "I'll be there in half an hour," he said. "Six months from now I'd be able to drive you. I'll have my driver's license then. I don't suppose you want to hang around that long?"

"Nope," I said. "When summer's over, I'm going home to Santa Barbara."

"You and the birds are flying south together," he said, laughing.

Birds, fluttering in panic over the stairs.

I'd heard them, and so had Molly.

Paul had killed his neighbor's birds.

Is that why I hear them? They're warning me? And Molly, too?

"Hey, you still there?" John D. demanded.

"Sure," I said. "I'm here."

"I thought you'd hung up."

"I'm going to, right now," I said. "See you in a few minutes."

After I said goodbye, I went back to the kitchen window and looked across the street at the new building. It was nice, in spite of being the place where Paul lived.

Why did I feel so bad about the building I was staying in, and not about the one across the street?

Could it be that something bad was going to happen here, and I could sense it coming?

That's really stupid, Kate, I told myself. Quit thinking like that.

John D. was five minutes early, and showed up carrying a large green umbrella printed with black frogs.

"What do you think?" he asked as he opened it in the hall to show me what it looked like.

"It's weird," I said. "But I like it, in a way."

"I got it at the zoo store. Are you ready to leave? Let's try the umbrella out and see if it works."

I locked the door behind me and pulled up my jacket hood. "Is it cold outside?"

"Nope, just wet."

We were halfway down the stairs when we heard Eloise and Molly above us, hurrying to catch up.

"Is that you I hear, John D.?" Molly yelled. "Did you take that tape back to the store yet?"

"I never had it!" John D. yelled back. "That kid drives me nuts," he told me.

Molly caught up with us. "Kate, don't go anywhere with him. Come with us instead. We're going to the dentist and you'll have more fun because he'll give you a pirate ring or a decoder pin if you let him do something to your teeth. It's great."

"Oh, sure!" John D. said, laughing.

"You look as if you're feeling better, Kate," Eloise said when she caught up, too.

"I really am," I said. "I'm going grocery shopping for Shelly. Can I pick up something for you?"

"Not a thing," Eloise said. "As soon as we're done at the dentist, I'll pick up some odds and ends on my way to Molly's sitter."

"Let me stay with Kate!" Molly howled. "She can babysit me while you work this afternoon."

"You're too much of a pest," Eloise said bluntly.

We had reached the door. Eloise and Molly hurried through the downpour in one direction, shouting their goodbyes, and John D. and I went in the other.

John D. opened the umbrella over us. "Great, huh?"

"Great," I said. I wasn't paying much attention to him because I'd seen a black car drive past and wondered for an instant if it was the one that had hit me. Seattle was a big city—there would be lots of black cars.

And some of the witnesses had thought the car had been dark green.

"John D., what kind of car does Paul drive?" I asked suddenly.

"Well, he's got an old one now, but when he first came here, he had a great one, a red sports job. I asked him why he got rid of it and he blew up all over me. I never did get an answer. Maybe he sold it because he needed the money. Medical school costs lots of bucks, Dad says."

We crossed the street together, stepping over the rain water that gushed in the gutter.

"I thought you said you didn't believe he was really going to medical school," I said.

"Yeah, but that's what he wrote on his lease. My dad got it out of his files the other night and forgot it on his desk, so I read it. He wrote on it that he was a medical student, and he filled in the questions about income by saying that his father paid his bills. And I guess it's true, because I remember my dad saying his rent is paid up two or three months in advance all the time."

"But then he wouldn't have needed to sell his car— if his father pays his bills," I said.

"Maybe he spends more than they give him, and he doesn't want to ask for more," John D. said.

I nodded. "Okay. But let's get back to the car he has now. Exactly what does this one look like?"

John D. stared at me. "It's black, just plain old black, with a few hundred rust marks on it. But why do you want to know? You wouldn't do anything crazy and go anywhere with him, would you? He's like the bogeyman! You wouldn't let him give you a ride, would you?"

"No!" I said. "But I couldn't help wondering . . ."

"If he was the one who hit you," John D. said, finishing the thought. "I wondered that, too. His car has more dents in it than I can count, so he could have hit you and everybody else in town. But it looked like that when he got it. There's no way of telling anything."

"Maybe some of the paint from Shelly's bike is still on it," I said. "If he was the one who hit me."

John D. nodded. "Yeah. I see what you mean. Did you tell the cops about him?"

"No," I said. "I can't stand him, but I don't have any real reason to think he was the one."

I didn't have a reason I could actually tell anybody, I thought. If I tried to explain my nightmares and those hallucinations (if that was what they were) when it seemed as if I was floating around Paul's apartment, anybody listening to me would think I was crazy.

And maybe I was. If I heard a story like that, wouldn't I think that the person telling it was imagining things?

I wanted to tell John D. about the nightmares, about all of it, but what could he do but laugh?

Or maybe he'd think that the accident had knocked my brains loose.

And he might tell his parents, who would have to tell Shelly . . .

And Shelly would have to call Dad over something as serious as that.

"You want me to show you Paul's car?" John D. asked. "We could look for paint chips."

I shook my head. "Better not," I said.

But I wondered if there was some way I could call

the police and not give my name when I asked them to go and look at Paul's car.

No. I didn't have that much courage. They could trace the call, even if I made it at a pay phone, and catch me before I got away. I'd learned that much from my spooky books and from television.

And when they caught me, they'd think I was a lunatic or a liar, because the only proof I had that Paul was the one who hit me was his own thoughts which I'd *heard*.

"I can just about believe Paul would run over you," John D. said. "He's mean enough. But why would he do it? Don't murderers usually have some sort of reason?"

Paul thinks he has one, I thought. He thinks Shelly brought me here to help her keep him away.

"Yes, I guess so," I said. I was sorry I'd started the conversation now. John D. had taken a bigger interest than I'd thought he would. "Hey, are you sharing that umbrella or using it to dump water on me?" I asked. "The overflow is getting me wetter than I would be if you didn't have it."

A car passed and splashed water on us, causing John D. to launch into a long description of how much better his life would be when he got a driver's license.

He seemed to have forgotten about Paul, and I'd had enough of talking about him, too. He scared me so much—but I couldn't think of any way to solve the problems he was creating. Not without creating even more problems for myself.

At the store, John D. helped me find the things on Shelly's grocery list and made a few suggestions that sounded pretty good to me.

When we finished there, we went next door to a small card shop, where I bought postcards to send home to Anne, who was watching my cat, and the neighbors who were taking care of our house.

John D., holding the grocery bags, waited while I scribbled a few words on the cards, sorted through the junk in my wallet until I found my stamps, and then dropped the cards in the mailbox on the corner.

On the way home, I held the umbrella over both of us. I liked his company, and I didn't want to be alone in the apartment, so I asked him if he wanted to have lunch with me.

"Sure," he said. "Or you could come over to my place. And we could stop and have a look at those puppies."

I wasn't up to meeting strangers, so I said we should stay at Shelly's apartment and keep out of the rain. That seemed to satisfy him.

While I fixed sandwiches for us, John D. climbed on a chair and tried to fix the cord on the curtain. I didn't ask him to do it, and I knew when he was done that he'd pull the curtain open.

"Don't open it, please," I said. "If Paul's home, he'll watch us and I don't like that." I tried to act casual, as if Paul's spying was only an annoyance and not something that scared me more than it angered me.

"Oh, yeah," John D. said as he fussed with the cord. "I forgot for a minute. But I don't think this is going to work anyway. Shelly needs a new cord, not one with a knot in it."

"Thanks for trying," I said. "Get down now and

help me set the table. Do you want one sandwich or two?''

''Two,'' he said. He stepped down from the chair and took the napkins I handed him. ''Or more,'' he added.

I spread butter on several slices of bread. ''Coming up,'' I told him. ''While I finish this, will you do me a favor?''

''Sure,'' he said.

''Tell me why you're called John D. and your father is called John C.''

''Oh, that,'' he said. He made a face. ''It's a really stupid family tradition.''

''I can see it's a tradition,'' I said. ''But why?''

''No, you can't see it,'' he said. ''You have to be outside to see it.''

''What are you talking about?'' I asked as I set a platter of sandwiches on the table.

''When we finish eating, walk outside with me and I'll show you.''

He wouldn't give me another hint.

When we finished lunch, we ran down the steps, out the front door, and across the street. Standing in the rain, John D. pointed up to the top floor of Shelly's building.

''See?'' he said. ''Look straight up from the front door to the ledge that runs around the building. See the lettering? Some of the vines have grown over part of it, but you can still read most of it.''

I squinted against the rain blowing in my face. ''I think it says John A. Perry,'' I said.

''He was my great-grandfather, and he built this place. But he didn't name his son John Jr. because he hated hearing kids called Junior. Instead, he started us through the alphabet. It's like a family curse.''

I couldn't help laughing. ''Is that true? I think it's the craziest story I ever heard.''

''Thank you very much,'' John D. said as he bowed to me. ''You're nice, too.'' He laughed a little and then said, ''I can't help what my family did to me. But that's not the worst of what you can see on this building. Look up again. Do you see something yellow up there?''

I saw something, but it was so small I'd never have noticed it if John D. hadn't pointed it out. ''What is it?'' I asked.

''My pocket radio,'' he said. ''Darn. I really liked it, too. It was waterproof, and it had a strap I could use to hang it from my bike.''

''How did it get up there?''

''Molly put it there,'' he said. ''I told you she's a brat. She took it off my bike one day when I was over here vacuuming, and the next thing I know, it's up there. She turned it on, too, with the volume on high, and it ran until the batteries went dead. Everybody was mad.''

He seemed to be more concerned about his radio than he was about little Molly crawling around on that ledge.

''I can't believe this,'' I said. ''Molly actually crawled out there and left your radio there? That's scary.''

''Not for her,'' John D. said bitterly. ''Heck, no. She just climbed out her bedroom window . . .'' He pointed to the far end of the building. ''See? The one that's second from the end. She crawled out and car-

99

ried my radio over to where you see it. Her mother won't let her go out again and get it, and nobody else wants to try, either. The nearest window is in your sister's apartment—maybe in the bedroom you're using. But you can't reach my radio. Shelly tried to snag it with my dad's fish net, but it was too far away. The noise was driving her and everybody else nuts. If Paul had been living across the street then, he probably would have torn down the building to get at the radio.''

It wasn't funny, not really. But I couldn't help laughing. ''What did you do to make Molly so mad?''

John D. threw up his hands. ''Who knows? She's got the worst temper of anybody I ever knew.''

''What are you doing out here?''

Paul's angry shout scared me out of my wits. I hadn't seen him coming, and I hadn't given him a thought for quite a while. But here he was, practically on top of us, and he looked as if he was ready to explode.

John D. only shrugged, stuck his hands in his pockets, and started across the street toward Shelly's building. For a moment, I seemed to have frozen in place, but finally I got hold of myself and tried to hurry after John D.

But Paul grabbed my arm and yanked it. ''I asked you a question,'' he said.

''I . . . I . . . I . . .'' I stuttered. I tried to twist loose from his grasp.

He let go of my arm abruptly and made a wild gesture. ''Get away from me. I hate freaks like you. I—I—I! Why don't you learn to talk?''

I ran away from him. John D. turned around at the

front door of Shelly's apartment house and waited for me.

"Jeez," he said as he shoved open the door. "He gets nuttier all the time. What did he say to you?"

"N-nothing," I said. "I can't remember."

I was shaking so hard that my teeth chattered. "Let's go upstairs," I said. "I'm cold."

John D. went up to the apartment with me, but he didn't stay. I couldn't blame him for wanting to go somewhere else. He made a feeble excuse about needing to check in with a friend of his about their plans for doing something together that night, and before I knew it, I was alone in the apartment.

I turned the TV on and sat down in front of it, trying to concentrate on the program. When the phone rang, part of me knew who it was.

"What were you doing out in front of my building?" Paul demanded.

"N-none of your business," I said.

Pull up your socks, Kate, I told myself fiercely. Don't let him hear you stutter or find out how scared you are. Take charge of your life for once. Do it!

"I won't tolerate you spying on me," he yelled into the phone. "I'll make you sorry."

I took a deep breath. "I'll tell my sister you're threatening me and she'll go to the police. We'll tell them all about you. Everything. They'll lock you up and then you'll be the one who's sorry."

I was so frightened that I could feel my knees trembling, but apparently Paul didn't realize that, because he yelled, "Don't you talk to me that way! Who do you think you are? I don't want you here. I want you to go back where you came from, and you'd better start packing now."

I took another deep breath. "If I left, it wouldn't do you any good," I said. "My sister despises you. She laughs at you. In a million years, she'd never let you come near her."

And I slammed down the phone.

I was shaking all over. When the phone began ringing again, I turned up the volume on the TV and let Paul hang up on the answering machine.

When Shelly got home that afternoon, she told me she'd made plans with Andy to see a movie that night.

I wanted to shout, "Don't leave me here alone!" But I didn't. I wanted her to ask me to go with them, but I don't think it occurred to her.

She didn't notice my distress—she was too excited about the date with Andy. I could have spoken up for myself. I could have told her about the phone call from Paul. But if I did that, then I'd have to tell her the rest of it or it wouldn't make any sense to her.

Actually, it wouldn't make any sense no matter how I explained the situation.

Andy showed up while Shelly was still getting ready. I was loading the dishwasher, and he leaned against the wall and talked to me while he waited. But I was barely listening. All I could think about was being left alone in the apartment with Paul across the street—and he'd probably know I was alone because he'd see my sister and Andy leave.

Then what?

After they left, I paced the floor for a few minutes. It wasn't dark yet, but I turned on all the lights anyway. I couldn't calm myself down enough to concentrate on TV or a book or radio music.

Finally I grabbed my key and headed down the hall to Eloise's apartment. Be home, I thought. Please be home so I don't have to be alone tonight.

I rang the bell, and Molly answered right away.

"Hey," she said. "Come on in and I'll show you the pirate ring the dentist gave me for not yelling in his office."

I slipped inside her apartment quickly.

"Who's that?" Eloise called from another room.

"It's Kate," Molly called back.

Eloise bustled in, rubbing lotion into her hands. "What can we do for you, Kate?"

I fidgeted miserably, and finally said, "Shelly went out to a movie with Andy, and I wondered—well . . ."

"Spend the evening with us," Eloise said. "We're going to make popcorn and watch the Cartoon Network. Is that exciting enough for you?"

An evening with popcorn and cartoons sounded like heaven. I followed Molly to the living room and sat down next to her on their couch.

As soon as her mother stepped into the kitchen, Molly leaned toward me.

"You're afraid to be alone, aren't you?" she whispered. "Because of him. That Paul. He's bad, you know. Really, really bad."

I felt better being there with her, because she understood. But she was only eight years old. She couldn't keep me safe. Maybe no one could.

Chapter Nine

"I'm glad you spent the evening with Eloise and Molly," Shelly told me the next morning at breakfast. "I'm embarrassed that I didn't think of sending you over there. In fact, I should have stayed home last night. I can't believe how selfish I was."

I didn't look up, but concentrated on the melon I was eating for breakfast. "You had a date," I said finally. "I don't know what got into me. Andy's really nice, and I don't blame you for going. I'm the one who's embarrassed for being such a baby."

Shelly sat down across from me. "No, you're not a baby. I was thoughtless."

"Forget about it," I said. "I had a good time with Eloise and Molly."

"You look like you didn't get much sleep last night," she said. "Headache again?"

"No," I said truthfully. "You don't look like you slept very well either."

"I had nightmares all night long," she said. "My guilty conscience was paying me back for leaving you here, I guess."

I had to laugh at that. "Well, you had a good time at the movie, didn't you?"

"No, actually I didn't. I worried and felt guilty all

evening, and then when I called after the movie was over and you didn't answer, I completely panicked and lost all my common sense. It was Andy who gave me the idea of calling to see if you'd gone over to see Eloise and Molly."

"Sorry I scared you," I said.

"Only for a minute," Shelly said. "As soon as I found you, everything was fine."

For you, maybe, I thought.

I had trouble keeping a smile on my face, but I didn't want to have hard feelings between us. I was certainly old enough to be left alone for an evening.

But if Shelly knew what I knew . . .

That wasn't fair. Even if I told her, she'd have trouble believing me. Maybe she wouldn't be able to believe me at all, and I couldn't imagine what might happen next, except that I was certain it would involve my parents. Immediately if not sooner. It would take a long time to outlive the way I'd acted last spring when the school counselor wouldn't believe me.

"Well, at least it's not raining today," I said. "You'll be able to drive to work."

Shelly laughed. "Are you reminding me that I'm a baby about some things, too?"

My face flushed. I hadn't been thinking about how afraid she was to drive in rainstorms.

"No, I was only making a comment," I said. "It's going to be a pretty day. Is it okay if I call John D. and see if he wants to do something?"

"Umm, what kind of something?" Shelly asked. "I know you're feeling better, but I don't think you should run around all day. Give me a call after you've talked to him, and let me know what your plans are, okay?''

''Okay,'' I said. While she hurried around getting ready for work, I turned on a morning TV show. I wasn't all that interested in it, but I wanted to hear some cheerful sounds in the apartment.

The news was on. I sat down on the couch to watch it as soon as I saw the start of a video clip made during rush hour the day before. A woman had been killed by a hit-and-run driver in the shopping district a few blocks away. The camera showed only a glimpse of someone covered with a blanket. All I could see of her through the pelting rain was a bit of her pink coat.

Her pink coat.

Shelly came into the living room, buttoning a dark blue jacket. ''What are you watching? You look like you've just seen a ghost.''

''Someone was killed by a hit-and-run driver in front of the grocery store where you shop,'' I said. My mouth was dry and my ears were ringing.

Shelly watched the man on TV talk about the accident. His face filled the screen, and she couldn't see what was behind him. She couldn't see the pink coat.

''That's awful,'' she said. ''Terrible. I'm going to call the police again this morning and ask if they know anything about the guy who hit you. What if this is the same man? Maybe he's a drunk or a drug addict—or just plain crazy.''

I cleared my throat. ''The dead woman was wearing a pink coat.''

Shelly stopped in her tracks. She touched her fingers to her mouth, as if to stop herself from speaking. Finally she asked, "Like mine?"

"I don't know. I only saw a little bit of it sticking out from under a blanket. It looked like the same color."

"I don't even want to wonder if it was the woman I saw with a coat like mine. She looked so friendly and nice. I'd hate to think of something awful happening to her."

Shelly! I wanted to scream. In that coat, maybe she looked like you!

Something else came on the TV then, so I turned it off. Tell her, I told myself. Ask her to stay home so you can tell her the whole thing.

"Shelly . . ." I began.

"I've got to rush," she said. She jingled her keys nervously and started for the door. "Remember, call me as soon as you talk to John D. I won't worry so much if I know what you're up to. And would you mind taking those steaks out of the freezer this afternoon?"

She was out the door and locking it behind her while I was still struggling with myself over whether or not to tell her what I knew about Paul.

Or what I thought I knew.

I paced the apartment again, going from window to window—except for the one in the dining room—to look across the street at Paul's apartment. His curtains were closed.

What had he done?

I stopped at the kitchen window and leaned over the sink.

What did you do? I thought as I stared at his apartment. I hurled my question at him, across the street and through the walls. *What did you do?*

But if he heard my challenge, he didn't respond. Instead, all I felt was a sense of great weight and an unexaminable darkness stretching ahead of me.

John D. called me before I had a chance to call him.

"The sun's out," he said. "How about going to the park? Or we can take a look at those puppies. Or . . ."

"John D., did you see the news this morning?" I asked quickly.

"News?" he asked. "No, I didn't see the news. Why would I watch something like that?"

"Somebody was run over in front of the grocery store yesterday," I said.

"Oh, yeah, I know about that. My mom drove by right after it happened. She said that the rain was falling so hard her windshield wipers didn't do much good, so maybe that's why the woman got hit."

"But the driver would have known he hit somebody!" I cried angrily. "Why didn't he stop?"

"Some people are creeps," John D. said. "Like the guy who hit you. Like Paul. So how about it, Kate? You want to go to the park or check out the pups?"

"Come on over and we'll decide then," I said. "I'll meet you downstairs in front."

John D. laughed. "You don't want Paul to see you leave, right?"

"I'd just as soon he didn't decide to go running on the same street we're using," I said, trying to make it sound casual.

When John D. hung up, I called Shelly and told her John D. and I were going out for a walk. It wasn't exactly the truth but it wasn't a complete lie, either. She told me to have a good time.

I grabbed a light jacket, just in case I'd need it. As I walked through the apartment, I checked out Paul's place through our windows again. The curtains were still closed, but that didn't mean he wasn't watching. At least he couldn't see me leave anymore, because the dining room window was still covered with the curtain. He might not know I was gone until I'd done what I had to do.

When John D. showed up, I didn't waste any time with small talk. "I want to see Paul's car for myself," I said.

John D. stared. "You mean you think you're going to find a big dent shaped like a body?"

"Maybe. Maybe that—and maybe a dent that looks like it was made when he hit a bike. Where does he park his car?"

John D. sighed. "I can't believe I'm letting you talk me into this crazy idea. Okay, he's got a slot in the underground garage, and you have to go around back to get in there. Or else you have to take the elevator down to the basement, and then . . ."

"No, no," I said hastily. I couldn't face the idea of accidentally ending up in an elevator with Paul, on the way to a dark basement and a parking garage.

"This is really dumb, you know," John D. said.

"Are you going to show me his car or not?" I demanded.

John D. sighed. "Okay, okay. But let's try not to attract any more attention than we have to. I'd hate for Dad to find out about this. And I definitely don't want to run into Paul again any time soon.''

We walked south a block, then circled around behind Paul's building. There were two big doors to the underground parking garage, and both were blocked by security gates.

''How are we supposed to get in here?'' I asked. I dreaded the idea of having to go inside the building and use the elevator.

John D. took a plastic card out of his pocket. ''With this,'' he said. He stuck one end of the card into a slot in a metal post beside one of the doors. The gate clanked back and John D. hurried in.

''Come on, come on,'' he said. ''I'm doing this under protest. If Paul comes down to get his car and catches me in here with you, I can bet my parents will hear about it within thirty seconds.''

''They didn't want you to go with me today?'' I asked, humiliated.

''They don't care if I go somewhere with you,'' John D. said. ''But I don't think a day in an underground parking garage is what they had in mind. It certainly wasn't what I had in mind.''

I sighed. ''Okay, okay. Just show me Paul's car. I'll check it out as fast as I can, and then we can leave.''

''It's over here,'' John D. said, and he trotted off toward a line of concrete pillars. Most of the parking places were empty at that time of the morning, but a few cars were still there. John D. was leading me toward the farthest corner of the garage.

''This is it,'' John D. said, and he pointed at an old black car with rusty spots and dozens of nicks and dents. "See? I told you there was no way of knowing if he's the one who hit you—not by checking for dents. From the way this car looks, he's hit every bike in Seattle. Maybe the police could test it and tell, but we sure can't."

I walked around the car twice. John D. was right. Either Paul was a terrible driver or he'd bought a car that was already beat up. It was a mess.

I spent a long time looking at the front bumper and the grill. Obviously he'd run into something, and not long ago, either, because the biggest dents didn't have rust showing or dirt lodged in them.

In fact, it was a surprisingly clean car. Of course, all the rain would have washed blood off, wouldn't it?

But then, according to the mysteries I'd read, it was possible for police labs to find even tiny spots of blood. Once I'd even read about an officer finding a single strand of hair that identified a certain car as the one that had killed someone. So it might be possible for the police to find evidence that would show that Paul had hit that woman in the pink raincoat. And maybe there'd be nearly invisible bits of paint from the bike I was riding, too.

But exactly how was I going to go about getting the police to look at Paul's car?

"You're making me nervous, scowling like that," John D. said.

"I'm making myself nervous," I said. "You're right—I can't tell anything by looking at these dents, but the police could."

"So why don't you call them and tell them what you think?"

I shook my head. "They wouldn't believe me. I don't have any proof."

Actually I was afraid to call the police. I remembered all too well what had happened when I tried to get help from the school counselor. Authority figures don't always act the way we want them to.

And if I called the police, Shelly would call my parents. They'd come home. Then what if it turned out that Paul hadn't done anything except act like a lunatic and scare me? I couldn't even count the number of times Mom had told me she wished I wouldn't read scary books because they would influence my thinking. Wouldn't she say that was what had happened to me? The books and those awful headaches I'd been having didn't give me much credibility.

"We'd better clear out," John D. said, looking around uneasily. "I keep expecting Paul to drop off the ceiling like a bat."

I laughed without wanting to, and my laughter echoed through the garage.

"Jeez, why don't you make some more noise?" John D. complained. "Maybe my dad'll hear it six blocks away and come running over and have me clean the floor in the laundry room again."

"Okay, let's leave," I said.

After we walked out, I watched while John D. stuck his plastic card into a slot on the post again, and the door shut. Elevators and covered parking. Why hadn't my sister moved into this building instead of the old one across the street? Even though she thought it was beautiful, it was still inconvenient.

And spooky. But then, she didn't think it was a scary building.

"You wasted your time, didn't you?" John D. said. "I told you there was no way you could tell anything. Unless you want to call the police, I don't know what else you can do. Like I said, Paul's a major jerk, but I don't think he'd actually hurt somebody."

Oh yes he would, I thought.

He's already done it.

But the sun was shining and the neighborhood was so beautiful, with all its old trees and wide flower gardens, that it wouldn't have taken much for me to once again brush everything off and blame my imagination.

We stopped by to see John D.'s friend and I played with the tiny gray puppies while their mother watched cheerfully. It was easy to forget I had any troubles then. I didn't even stutter.

But when we got back to the apartment house, I began feeling awful again. A fist seemed to tighten around my stomach. The building that Shelly thought was so pretty reminded me of a haunted house. Even the sight of John D.'s pocket radio high up on the ledge over the main entrance didn't amuse me.

"Do you want to come in?" I asked, anxious not to be left alone. "I can fix us something to eat."

"Nope, but thanks anyway," John D. said. "I've got some stuff I've got to do. Maybe we can get together later today."

I watched him leave and wanted to run after him. I didn't want to be alone.

I climbed the stairs slowly, reluctantly. It had been warm outside. Inside, the air seemed damp and cold.

I hunched my shoulders, expecting to hear the birds again, but I didn't.

I felt suddenly tired and incredibly stupid. What had I learned by making John D. show me Paul's car? Only that he had a crummy old car.

The real truth was that I still didn't have any proof that Paul was dangerous. Everybody except Molly and me thought he was a jerk, nothing more.

What did Molly know? More than I, I suspected. And more than that awful business about the cat. She was keeping secrets, too. Why? Why couldn't she tell her mother? I didn't know Eloise very well, but I was certain that if she had any idea Molly was scared, she'd do something.

Maybe Molly had the answers I needed. But did she trust me enough to confide in me?

On impulse, when I reached the top floor I turned toward Eloise's apartment instead of Shelly's. When I rang the bell, I could hear Molly hollering inside.

Her mother answered the door. "Oh, Kate! This is nice. I'm always glad to see you, but I have to leave for the bookstore in a few minutes, and we're rushing around getting ready. Come in anyway, though. You can keep Molly out of my hair while I finish up."

Molly, still in her underwear, appeared in their bathroom doorway holding a toothbrush. "Is it hot outside?" she asked. "I don't need jeans and a sweater, do I? I can wear shorts, can't I?"

"I guess you'd better wear whatever your mom's got planned for you," I said. "Seattle weather can be tricky."

Molly disappeared through another door and came back, pulling a dark blue sweatshirt over her red hair.

"Mom, why don't I stay with Kate instead of going to day camp. I'm tired of it. I want to stay with Kate."

"No, no," Eloise said. She yanked a brush through her daughter's hair, scowling at her. "Don't start with that again. Your friends are expecting you so that's where you're going."

"I don't have any friends there!" Molly said. "I hate everybody and everybody hates me."

"Well, that's a recommendation to Kate, isn't it?" Eloise said. "Why would she want to baby-sit you after you say something like that?"

"Actually, I'd love to baby-sit," I said. "Here or in Shelly's apartment."

"I want to go to the park!" Molly bellowed. "I want to go to the ice cream shop!"

Eloise rolled her eyes. "Kate, are you sure about this?"

"Sure," I said. "Just tell me where you want her and what you want us to do."

"She needs lunch, so maybe you could start here. But call the store and let me know where you plan on ending up."

"Sure," I said again. Molly and I had quite a few things in common. Both of us had to account for our time.

And both of us were afraid of Paul.

Eloise left, still issuing instructions to Molly about how she was to behave, what she could and could not say—"Don't say one word about Mrs. Carroll's wart if you see her!"—and how much ice cream she could have. When the door shut, Molly sighed.

"Don't you hate it when they do that?" she asked.

I nodded. "But I think that's part of being a mother," I said.

"Or a big sister, like Shelly," Molly said. "Nag, nag. Well, why don't we have lunch now? Then we can go somewhere."

"I'd better call Shelly first," I said. "She'll want to know where I am."

"That's because she thinks you hurt your brain," Molly said.

I was reaching for Eloise's phone when I heard Molly say that, and I froze for a moment. Finally I managed to ask Molly what she'd said. I wasn't certain I'd heard her right.

"Shelly thinks you hurt your brain when you got knocked off your bike the other day," Molly said. She climbed on a kitchen stool and smiled at me. "Sorry, but I forget what she called it."

"A concussion," I said. "But the doctor said I didn't have one."

"Yeah, but Shelly thinks you did, because you have bad headaches and yell in your sleep. She was going to take you back to the doctor, but you seemed to get better, so she said she'd wait and see."

Great, I thought. Shelly's been talking about me behind my back.

Well, who could blame her for that? I could feel a blush burning my face.

"But Mom said maybe it's too much, being in a strange place and getting hurt, too, and so maybe you're only nervous."

Nervous. Well, who wouldn't be?

"I'm fine now," I told Molly.

Molly shook her head slowly. "Maybe you aren't

hurt anymore, but Paul hates you, and nobody can be fine if Paul hates them.''

Here was my chance. ''Like you?'' I said quickly. ''Paul doesn't seem to like you very much, either, so are you saying that you don't think you're 'fine'?''

Molly blinked twice, opened her mouth, and then shut it again. Before I could protest, she took off down the hall.

''Hey, what's wrong?'' I called out. But Molly didn't answer.

Obviously I'd have to wait and try later to find out what had happened to Molly. But seeing her reaction to my curiosity bothered me a lot.

I called Shelly at her office and told her I was babysitting Molly for the afternoon.

''She's quite a handful,'' my sister said. ''Are you sure you want to do this?''

''I'm already doing it,'' I said. ''I'll fix her lunch first, and then we'll go out for a while.''

''Call me when you get back,'' Shelly said.

I promised I would. When I checked out the kitchen, I found lots of things that I could make sandwiches with, but I didn't know what Molly liked, so I followed her down the hall and found her in her bedroom, sitting on the edge of her bed.

''Are you okay?'' I asked. She looked a little grim.

She nodded and said, ''Of course. But I don't want to talk about Paul anymore.''

''Okay. I'd rather have lunch. How about you? What sort of sandwich do you like?''

''Peanut butter,'' she said.

''But there's all sorts of other stuff,'' I said. ''Are you sure that's all you want?''

"I like peanut butter best."

"You've got it, then. Come on out and set the table for me." I put on my biggest smile, but Molly wasn't impressed.

"You're still thinking about Paul," she said. "Quit it. You make me think of him."

She was reading my mind again.

"Okay," I said. "I'll do my best. But I don't know as much about him as I want to, and I was hoping you'd help. I really need your help."

"No," Molly said. "Let's go eat lunch."

And that was that. Molly was as stubborn as a kid can get.

I was tired by the time I said goodbye to Molly late that afternoon. Shelly was already home when I reached her apartment, rattling pans in the kitchen and humming to herself.

"I got salmon at the store," she said. "I hope you like it."

"I love it. Can I help with anything?"

Shelly glanced over at me. "Hey. You look exhausted. Molly must have run your legs off this afternoon."

"Close," I said. "But I can still fix a salad."

"Go lie down instead. I hate seeing you so pale. I'll call you when dinner's ready."

I shuffled down the hall, feeling more exhausted every moment. As soon as I reached my room, I pulled the curtain closed. It was becoming an automatic gesture.

When I stretched out on the bed, I shut my eyes

and did my best to relax. So tired, I thought. How did I get so tired?

I drifted into a half-dream state. A long hall seemed to stretch before me. Suddenly a door at the end opened, and a dark figure was silhouetted against a blinding light.

Why were you here? Why were you snooping around my building?

I was too frightened to speak. How had Paul found out I'd been in his building?

You can't hide from me! If you don't leave me alone, I'll kill you! Do you understand? I'll kill you!

I struggled to wake, and found myself sitting up, gasping for breath.

I'll kill you both!

Even awake, I could hear him.

Chapter Ten

When Shelly called me for dinner, I didn't want to eat. All I wanted to do was run.

There was no way I could tell her what was happening, because there was no way she'd believe me. I was certain of that, after what Molly had said earlier in the day about Shelly thinking I had a concussion.

What would Shelly do if I said I could hear Paul's thoughts, and he wanted to kill us both? She wouldn't have much choice. She'd have to call a doctor—and our dad. And then what?

"Not hungry?" Shelly asked as I picked at my food.

"Sure I am," I said as heartily as I could. "I love salmon." I chewed and swallowed food I couldn't taste, and hoped she wouldn't ask me any more questions.

"What about the headaches?" she asked.

"I don't have them anymore," I said. "My arm's still sore, though, but not like it was." I held it up so she could see the scraped place. "Ugly, right?"

"Not too pretty," she said. "But you're lucky you didn't break anything."

No thanks to Paul, I thought. "Have you talked to

the police again? You said you'd call because of the woman who was killed.''

''I did call,'' Shelly said. She took a sip of water, as if she wanted to delay telling me. ''They didn't see any connection at all between the woman who was killed and your being knocked off your bike. But they didn't say the idea was stupid, either.''

''But I've dropped off their list, pretty much. Right?'' It took all the strength I could manage not to burst into tears.

Shelly sighed. ''The man I talked to didn't say that, not exactly, anyway. It makes me angry. If the same drunk driver did it—well, maybe they could have saved a life if they'd paid more attention to us.''

I didn't know what to say. The truth—or what sometimes seemed to me to be the truth—wouldn't get an appreciative audience anywhere.

It suddenly dawned on me that maybe people would even laugh at me.

Rain began falling while we had our dessert. It was only a light rain, but it seemed so depressing we went around closing curtains so we wouldn't have to look at it. Of course, the dining room curtain was still closed. Shelly never even talked about fixing the cord anymore.

We went to bed early, even though it was Friday night. I was afraid I'd fall asleep and dream about Paul.

But I was afraid to stay awake, too, because Paul's thoughts sometimes overpowered me.

I tried to read, but I was so apprehensive that I had trouble concentrating, so finally I gave up.

Knotted with anxiety, I stared at the ceiling. I was

determined to stay awake, but exhaustion dragged me down and a sick sleep rolled over me.

In my dreams, a dark street stretched out, wet and shining, lined with heavy, dripping trees, and behind the trees there were houses, closed against the night. I ran lightly, free from fear, behind a dark dream runner, and he was unaware of my presence.

I matched his easy, loping stride, following him tirelessly. I was a dreamer observing my dream, without the uproar of involvement.

The runner never looked up, but instead he concentrated on his stride, and evil flicked off him like hissing sparks.

As he passed each house, lights flared in bedroom windows and helpless sleepers, stung awake by night fright, cried aloud.

But I, the creator of the dream, was safe from him.

But then I found myself ahead of him in some appointed place, facing him, watching him bear down on me. Now I was involved! Now I was terrified and unable to move!

The runner grinned.

I jerked upright, wide awake. The headache was back, roaring and drumming. I pressed my hands to my head, trying to absorb the agony.

He's coming, I thought. Paul. He's out there, somewhere in the city, and he's padding toward me, always padding toward me. He could catch me unaware, and I'd be helpless.

Or he'd catch my sister. And she didn't know he existed. She only knew about ugly, mean-spirited Paul, not the runner, that other part of him, who meant us harm.

Who meant to kill us.

And there was nothing between him and my sister except me.

I lay awake the rest of the night, waiting. I wasn't certain what I was waiting for, but I was afraid.

But nothing happened. I didn't hear Paul's thoughts or drift helplessly into his room. I didn't follow him on the streets again. I simply waited—and perhaps that was harder than anything else.

My parents called the next morning while we were eating breakfast. It hadn't even been a week since I last talked to them, but I was so glad to hear their voices that I nearly cried.

"How are you?" Mom asked immediately.

"I'm fine," I said. I stared hard at Shelly so she'd pick up on what I was saying. "I feel just great. Seattle must agree with me. How about you and Dad? What have you guys been doing?"

While Mom described their trip so far, I wondered what would have happened if I'd gone with them. I wished I had, except that then Shelly would have been alone in Seattle with crazy Paul across the street.

Dad came on the line next, and after we talked for half a minute, he asked for Shelly. When I handed her the phone, I whispered, "I'm fine!" Shelly nodded.

When Dad hung up, Shelly said, "They sound great, don't they?"

I nodded. It was only June, and Mom and Dad would be gone for weeks. How could I stand it for that long?

*   *   *

Shelly had planned to spend the day driving me around Seattle, showing me the sights. Before we left, Eloise came by and showed Shelly two concert tickets for Sunday night.

"My favorite customer gave them to me," she said. "She and her husband can't go. Do you want to go with me? I can get a sitter . . ."

"I hate leaving Kate alone at night," Shelly said.

"Let me baby-sit Molly and then I won't be alone," I said quickly. I didn't want Shelly to be stuck at home with me, and I'd have another chance to see if I could find out what had happened between Molly and Paul.

"Are you sure?" Eloise said. "She can be an absolute beast."

"I think she's terrific," I said.

"But would you mind staying at our place?" Eloise asked. "That way she can go to bed at a decent time."

Ha, I thought. I was certain Molly would go to bed whenever she felt like it.

"I'd be glad to," I said.

"You're sure?" Shelly asked.

"Shelly! I'm positive!" I said.

Maybe it was a dumb idea, but it seemed to me that my best source of help right then was an eight-year-old.

Shelly and I left a few minutes later. I wasn't exactly happy about going out the back door where Paul could see us, but his curtains were closed and that reassured me a little.

The sky was overcast when we started out, but by noon the sun was shining. That cheered me up. We were looking for a parking place on the waterfront when Shelly said, "There. That's the smile I've been waiting to see."

I had to laugh. She was right. Smiling had been hard for me the last few days.

"There's a store here that I know you'll love," Shelly said. "If I can only find a place to park! And then we'll have lunch. Okay?"

"Perfect."

We found a spot to park on the next block, and began walking back to the import store Shelly had pointed out. Suddenly I felt overwhelmed with cold. The sun was still shining, but I was covered with goosebumps. The faces of the people we passed all seemed threatening. The gulls overhead swooped too low and screamed too loud.

Where are they? Shelly's car is gone! Where did they go? This is Kate's doing. She's persecuting me, invading me, spying on me. She's ruined everything. If it wasn't for her, Shelly would have cared for me. She would have understood me. She wouldn't be sneaking around with her sister. Where are you? Where are you?

I staggered and nearly fell. Paul knew we were gone and he was furious. Fractured images crowded my mind. Paul riding up in an elevator, with a woman staring at him and then turning away, pale with fright. Paul bursting through his door, into the bare room. Twisting his head around, startled when he heard a sound. Something was pecking and scratching on his wall, and a small hole appeared. Deep inside, he saw a tiny sharp beak and two bright eyes. Then, when he jumped back, the hole disappeared.

You're playing tricks on me, Kate! I'll stop you! I'll stop you!

I gasped.

"What's wrong?" Shelly asked.

"Nothing," I said quickly. My mouth was dry and my voice sounded strange. "I just got a twinge in my arm."

"Are you sure you're all right?" Shelly asked.

"Hey, don't fuss," I said. "Isn't this the store? Let's go in. It looks like fun."

I pushed through the door ahead of Shelly. "Come on, sis," I urged her.

She laughed at me and hurried along behind. "Now you're acting like a tourist. Good."

I smiled and looked around blindly. "It's about time," I said.

We didn't get home until late that evening. As soon as I got out of Shelly's car, I looked up at Paul's windows. The curtains were closed, but I had a strong feeling that he wasn't there. Maybe he'd been out looking for us.

We found a note from John D. taped to the apartment door.

"*Kate, call me immediately!!!!*" he had written.

Inside, the light on the answering machine was blinking. Shelly played back the messages and stared at me while John D.'s voice said over and over, "Kate, call me right away," or "Kate, call me the second you get home," or "Kate, where are you? I have to talk to you."

"What's that all about?" Shelly asked. "He sounds as if he's in a complete panic."

He did sound that way, but I didn't want Shelly getting too curious.

"Oh, you know John D.," I said. "He probably had a fight with Molly at the video store and wants to tell me his side before she can tell me hers."

Shelly laughed as she pulled off her jacket. "Go ahead and call him. I can't wait to find out what he wants."

I hated calling John D. while Shelly was still in the room, but I didn't have a choice. I looked up his number in her phone book, called, and waited while the phone rang several times. Finally an answering machine came on the line.

"It's Kate, John D.," I said after I heard the beep. "I'm returning your call."

When I hung up, Shelly looked disappointed. "Darn it," she said. "I wonder what's going on."

"Nothing much, I bet," I said. I tried to look as casual as I could when I went down the hall to my room. As soon as I closed my door behind me, I let out the breath I'd been holding.

What's happened, John D., I wondered. Why do you sound so worried?

I heard the phone ring and opened my door again, expecting Shelly to tell me that John D. was on the line. Instead, I heard her say, "Hi, Andy." She sounded really happy that he'd called.

I closed my door and sat down on the bed. John D. was still on my mind. What could be so important?

Shelly rapped on my door. "Hey, Kate? Do you want to go to a movie with Andy and me tonight?"

My first impulse was to shout "Yes!" Anything to get out of this apartment and away from the building that seemed so gloomy to me. And the more distance I put between Paul and me, the better off I'd be.

But then, what about John D.?

I opened my door again. "Gee, Shelly, I don't think Andy really wants me along. You go without me, and have a good time."

"I can't leave you here alone," Shelly said. "I made one horrible mistake and I'm not making another."

I shrugged. "Hey, maybe Eloise and Molly are home. Or I can keep trying John D. and invite him over."

Shelly grimaced. "No, no, that won't do at all. I'll feel guilty or worry so much I won't be able to enjoy the movie. Say you'll come. I'm sure you'll like it."

She didn't leave me much choice. "Okay," I said.

As soon as she got off the phone, I tried John D. again. He still wasn't home, but since Shelly wasn't in the room, I left another message. "John D., I have to go out with Shelly tonight," I said. "Call me the very first thing tomorrow morning, before you do anything else."

I didn't want John D. to get the idea that I didn't care about his messages, but I didn't want his parents to wonder too much about my call.

Halfway through the movie, the deep cold I'd learned to dread swept over me again, and I gritted my teeth. Paul was thinking about Shelly and me again.

In my mind, I saw him running again, without effort, filling his lungs with damp, clean air. He ran on sidewalks that were shining and wet, and as he approached each street light, his thin shadow pulled short, gathered under him, and then shot out ahead, pointing his way.

There were other people out on the streets where he ran, but he never saw them draw back as he passed, look after him, and then hurry on, their shoulders knotted protectively.

He passed a small house with a child's toys on the front porch. Inside, the child woke suddenly and sat upright, staring into the darkness in her room. She tumbled out of bed, screaming for her mother.

Farther down the block, a young artist bent over paper tacked to a heavy board. The watercolor wash was almost dry. Carefully, she loaded her brush with the colors that would have brought to life tree trunks and bare branches on some other night, but her hand would not obey her, and the thin dark figure of a runner flowed out beneath the sable hairs. She blinked and stared. The brush moved toward the metal tray that held her colors, touched it, and moved back. A bright red splotch leaked out on the damp paper. She blinked again, sickened by what she saw, and called out her husband's name in a voice he did not recognize. Neither of them heard the runner, quietly padding past.

The neighborhood dogs did not warn off the intruder. Old memories stirred and an ancient order of dominance reestablished itself. This predator would not be challenged by them.

Shelly. Where did you and Kate go with him tonight? Where? What plans are you making? How much do you know?

He knew we'd gone out with Andy. His thoughts

were stronger than ever. But I could see and hear him better than ever, too. Did that mean both of us were gaining power?

Could I protect us from him?

I remembered the wall I'd built around myself to keep his thoughts away. Could I surround him with it and make him feel my presence and my power?

In my mind, I raised a black wall that stretched beside him as he ran. He glanced at it—then stopped.

And then he turned back and stared at me.

Kate, get away from me!

I nearly retreated. But instead, I forced the black wall higher, and began raising another on the other side of him. Now I had created a tunnel. He turned suddenly and began running through it.

I slammed a wall across the end. He stopped and faced me again.

I'll make you sorry.

"No, I'll make YOU sorry!" I shouted back at him from in my mind. "Watch me!"

I slammed down another wall, closing him in.

"You can't get out until I let you out," I told him.

I waited, and when he screamed with rage, I gasped.

"Kate?" Shelly touched my arm. "You okay?"

I took a deep breath. "The movie's a little noisy sometimes," I said.

She nodded. On the other side of her, Andy leaned forward to look at me, seemed to be reassured, and looked back at the screen.

The night scene I'd been watching in my mind had disappeared. I felt around mentally, trying to see if

Paul was still listening to my thoughts or sensing me. All I felt was blankness.

I was exhausted.

When we got home, Andy left us off in front. Upstairs, we found two more messages from John D. Both said the same thing. "Aren't you home yet?"

"He's certainly persistent," Shelly said. "I wonder what's on his mind."

"Probably Molly and her mother checked out every video he wanted to watch tonight," I said, and I tried to laugh. It didn't sound all that great, so I added, "Gosh, I'm tired. I'm going to bed right now."

"Good idea," Shelly said.

The last thing I did before I crawled into bed was look across the street at Paul's apartment. The curtains were closed but the lights were on.

I didn't want another battle of the minds with him, so I spent a while constructing a giant mental wall around myself.

You can't get in, Paul, I thought. You'll die if you try. You'll die.

For a moment, it seemed to me that I heard Paul's mad shouts somewhere in the distance, so far away that I couldn't make out the words.

I slammed another, higher wall around me, and the last of his shouts was cut off.

But I was so tired, so tired, and all I wanted was to be free of this battle I'd never asked for.

Paul was getting crazier every day. If this went on much longer, I'd have to tell Shelly and take my chances with what she'd do. Could I ever convince her that Paul might have been the one who ran over the woman outside the grocery store?

Was there a way I could tell the story and leave out my ability to read Paul's mind?

Or was there a way I could prove it?

Chapter Eleven

In a dimly lit room, I drifted under the ceiling, and a dozen small birds glided soundlessly with me. Sometimes their wings brushed against me, but they weren't alarmed by this contact. Even though they were flying, they seemed as if they were sleeping.

Below me, the dark runner lay back, exhausted. His tan eyes stared. His thin hair was wet with sweat.

Suddenly he pushed himself up to a sitting position and looked around. "You mind your own business," he muttered. "You let me alone."

The birds became agitated when they heard his voice. Their high-pitched cries filled the room.

"Who's here?" the runner cried. "Who is it? Is that you, Kate? Shelly?"

I concentrated on escape, willing myself across the room and through the walls. I had as much power as Paul, or maybe even more, but I was afraid.

Go, go, I told myself. Get out of here!

Light exploded, the birds shrieked, and I found myself in my own bed.

And then I heard Shelly cry out.

I leaped out of bed and ran down the hall, calling

out her name. Someone was here! Someone was hurting Shelly!

But in the glow cast by her bedside light, I saw Shelly sitting up, groggy and pale, with a book open beside her. No one else was there.

"What's wrong?" I cried.

She shook her head and seemed bewildered. "I must have fallen asleep while I was reading. I had the most horrible dream." She closed her eyes and pressed her fingers against her mouth. "Horrible."

I sat down on the edge of the bed. "Can I do something for you? I hate nightmares. I'm always afraid to fall back asleep."

"I know what you mean. It was the worst nightmare I've ever had."

I was afraid to learn what she'd dreamed, but I had to ask. "What was it?"

She laughed a little. "It sounds stupid now," she said. "I dreamed I was in a car during a rainstorm—I wasn't driving—and a woman in a raincoat like mine stepped off the curb. There was plenty of time to stop, but the driver of the car speeded up instead and hit her deliberately. I couldn't prevent it. It all seemed so real! I felt so helpless."

I was stunned. Had the accident been worrying her privately so much that she was now dreaming about it? Or was she, too, reading Paul's mind and discovering that he had been the one who hit that woman?

"Why don't I fix us both some herbal tea?" I asked. "I saw some in your cupboard. Does that sound good?"

She threw back her blankets. "I should be the one taking care of you," she said.

"Maybe both of us should get up, have the tea, and then try going to bed all over again," I suggested.

Shelly looked at her watch and laughed. "It's two-thirty. Why not have the tea? We can't be worse off than we are now."

We drank our tea in the living room—I didn't want to sit at the dining room table. Maybe it was only a few feet closer to Paul, but even that was too much.

When we were done, we went back to our rooms. Both of us left our lights on.

In the morning, I called John D. as soon as I got up. Luckily for both of us, he answered.

"Where were you when I called?" he demanded.

"Where were *you*?" I demanded right back.

"I went to my grandfather's birthday party last night," he said. "But before that . . ."

He stopped talking suddenly.

"You still there?" I asked.

"Uh, hey, why don't we get together this morning and go see those puppies again?" he said.

"They were cute, John D., but . . ."

"Sure, nine-thirty is fine with me, too," he said.

"Hey!" I protested. "I'm missing something. What are you talking about?"

"See you out *front* of your place," he said, and then he hung up.

" 'Bye," I said to a dead line.

"What was so important to John D.?" Shelly asked, as she came into the room.

"You know him—he's weird sometimes," I said vaguely.

That comment usually satisfies adults where teenagers are concerned.

"He wants to go see his friend's puppies again," I added. "Well, they are pretty cute. Is that all right with you?"

Shelly groaned. "I think puppies are cute, too, but I don't think I'd want to look at any this early in the morning. I'm wondering if I'm going to make it to the concert with Eloise tonight."

"Go back to bed," I said. "Sleep until noon. Then you'll feel great."

I only said that because it was her apartment and she loved it. There was no way I'd be able to take a nap in that building. It was still too creepy for me. Even if I managed to solve the problems Paul created, I wasn't certain I wanted to spend the rest of the summer there with my sister.

Shelly took my advice and went back to bed. I fixed myself a breakfast of fruit and cereal, showered, and got dressed in time to meet John D. in front of the building at nine-thirty.

"Okay," I said the moment I saw him. "What's been going on?"

He was so excited about what he was going to tell me that he couldn't stand still. "Listen, this will knock you over," he said. "Crazy Paul has a new car. I mean a different car. He got rid of the black one with all the dents, and now he's got a gray one, a compact, and it's in better shape but it's not new, either."

Two elderly women leaving the building stared at him as they passed.

"Let's walk up the street while we're talking," I said. "I feel conspicuous here."

John D. and I walked along for a few feet before I looked around to be sure no one could hear me, and then I said, "I bet he got rid of the car in case the police ever want to check it out."

"That's what I thought, too," John D. said. "There's been a lot on the TV news programs about that woman who was killed. Have you been watching?"

"Me? No, and I thought you weren't interested in the news either," I said.

"My whole family is interested in the woman, because it turns out that she was a teacher at the same school where my mom's going to be teaching next fall."

"Your mom knew her?" I asked.

"No, no, she didn't know her," John D. said. "But you can see that she'd be interested."

"You didn't tell your parents that I think Paul ran over her?" I asked, ready to be very, very upset if he had done something like that.

"No!" John D. said. "They'd think I was nuts."

"They'd think I'm nuts, too," I said. I gave John D. a long look. "How did you find out about the car?"

"I was sweeping the sidewalk by the doors to the parking garage, when out he came. He practically ran over me when he was leaving the garage. I didn't see him return, but before I went to Grampa's party, I came back and had a look. The same gray car was parked in his slot. It's maybe five years old and in fairly good shape, but there's some junk in the back seat. I tried to see as much of it as I could through the windows—most of it looks like trash. But I did see the big label on a brown shipping bag.''

''There was a name?'' I asked quickly.

''Yeah. Alvin King. Same last name.''

''Do you think that Paul borrowed the car from a relative?'' I asked.

''I bet he did. Probably he made some excuse about his car needing repair work so he could borrow it.''

''Then where do you suppose his black car is?''

John D. shrugged. ''I bet he ditched it, because according to the news, the police are looking hard for the car that killed that woman.''

''He'd better not get away with anything,'' I said angrily. ''I'm sick of him. I hate dreaming about him all the time and knowing what he's thinking . . .''

''What?'' John D. asked. He gawked at me.

My face burned. ''I know he hates me,'' I stuttered. ''He's jealous of everybody around Shelly.''

''Oh, yeah,'' John D. said. ''Yeah.''

I had to be more careful.

John D. and I did go to see the puppies. He really wanted to, and I guess I did, too—they were so cute. Sometimes it's nice to concentrate on something that's normal and cheerful.

On the way back to Shelly's, I suddenly had a brilliant idea.

''Do you have a key to Paul's apartment?'' I asked.

''Hey, no,'' John D. said. ''My parents have master keys that fit all the apartments, but I never use them. I don't have a reason to.''

"But could you get one and look around inside Paul's apartment if you had to?"

He stared at me again. "I don't *have* to," he said. "Why would I do that? I saw the place lots of times when he used to make me run all those errands for him."

"Maybe something's different," I said. "Maybe you could find out something about this Alvin King, like where he lives. We could go look and see if the black car was there."

"But what if it is there?" John D. asked. "To get Paul blamed for killing that woman, we'd have to let the police know about the car. You said you didn't want to talk to them because they wouldn't believe you."

"Probably they won't," I said. "I'm a teenager, and Paul would just say I had a grudge against him. But we could write a letter and not sign it."

"We could," John D. said. "And there's a number they keep showing on the news for people who want to tell suspicious stuff to the police but don't want to be involved. But they'd probably trace the number. I bet they've got Caller I.D."

"We could call from a pay phone," I said.

"That would show up, too. Maybe they'd send out a police car and grab you while you were still talking."

I bit my lip. I'd read more than once about things like that happening.

"I guess it's possible," I said. "But if they'd do all of that, why do they ask people to call the number?"

"Who knows why anybody does anything," John

D. said. "But if I were you, I'd take a chance and call them up. I'd come right out and say he ran over you and you're sure he ran over that woman, too. If they think you made it up, well, at least you tried."

"Shelly already told them that," I said. "They didn't think she was right."

"She said she *knew* he'd killed that woman?"

"No, no, she just said she thought he could be the one, because both things happened in the same neighborhood. She doesn't really know for sure he did it, you know. She doesn't even know for sure he hit me."

John D. shrugged. "Actually, neither do you. Not when it comes right down to it."

I opened my mouth and shut it again. There was no way I could risk telling John D. how much I knew and how I'd learned it. And I sure didn't want to explain that I wasn't ready to get into a lot of trouble again with authority figures who'd rather squash the messenger than listen to the message. There had been boys at my school who would handle a monster like Bernie by simply punching her out. They sure wouldn't go home and bawl for days the way I did.

"Look," I said finally. "Maybe if you go into his apartment, you can find something that would help us figure him out."

"Why don't you do it?" he asked. "Maybe—probably—I could get a master key. There's always one in the custodian's cupboard and he leaves it unlocked no matter how many times Dad tells him not to. I'll just borrow it for a while and then let you in. You know what will help you better than I do."

I was too scared to go in Paul's apartment. I was

absolutely certain that he would somehow sense it if I snooped through his things. He knew when my mind was there, so why wouldn't he know when my body was?

I shook my head hard and told John D. part of the truth. "I'm too scared to do that," I said. "What if he came home? He'd do something awful to me. But if it was you he caught . . ."

"He'd do something awful to me," John D. finished. "Like tell my dad. Then I won't get my driver's license until I'm thirty-five."

"You could make an excuse," I said. "You could say you heard strange noises and thought maybe a burglar was in Paul's apartment."

"So why didn't I call 911 then?" John D. asked. "That'll be the first thing anybody asks."

"Okay, you could say you heard water running and thought maybe he had a leaky pipe."

"You think anybody would believe that I'm always wandering around the halls with a master key, listening for running water? Listen, Kate, this guy goes crazy over stuff that nobody else cares about. What do you think he'd do if he caught me in his apartment?"

I sighed. "Okay. He'd probably throw you off his balcony. How about this? What if I talk Shelly into taking me out to lunch and make a big fuss about leaving, so Paul sees us for sure. He might follow us. You'd know if he did. When you see him leave, go into his apartment and have a good look."

John D. made a face. "I think I'm going to get in serious trouble before this is over."

"Only if you get caught," I said.

"Are you sure you're not related to Molly?" he asked. "This sounds like something she'd do."

"Will you try it?" I asked.

He agreed, but not very cheerfully. "Call me if you figure out a way to get your sister to take you out to lunch. I know I can get a key, but right now I'm wishing I'd never told you there was such a thing as a master key. When I've got it, I'll come back and watch, and if I can, I'll have a look around his place. But if I get caught . . ."

"I'll send flowers," I said, trying to make him laugh.

He didn't.

When I got home, I found Shelly wrapped in a towel and drying her hair in the bathroom.

"Do you feel better now?" I asked.

"Lots," she said.

"You want to feel good for tonight, so why don't we go out for lunch and maybe have takeout for dinner? I'll treat us. It's about time I spent a little more of the money Mom gave me."

Shelly grinned. "Far be it from me to turn down a free meal. Do you have a place in mind for lunch?"

"I don't know many restaurants here, so I'll let you choose. But let's pick one on the other side of town, so I have a chance to see more of Seattle."

"I know a wonderful place," she said. "It's an outdoor café, and the weather looks nice this morning. They open at eleven-thirty. How about that?"

"Perfect," I said.

While she finished her hair, I sneaked down the hall to phone John D. in the living room. I told him we'd be leaving soon and wouldn't be back for a long time. Then, before Shelly caught me, I hung up.

My heart was beating hard. I was scared for John D., but I was scared for me, too.

Now I had to do whatever I could to make sure Paul knew we were leaving. I went back to my room and spent a long time fussing with my curtain. Then I opened my window and leaned out, looking back and forth at the street below, taking my time. I leaned out a little farther and tried to see John D.'s radio on the ledge under his great-grandfather's name, but it was out of sight. Every once in a while I'd take a quick look across the street at Paul's windows, and finally I was rewarded when I saw one of his curtains move.

He tore it open so suddenly and startled me so much that I practically fell out the window. There he was, looking straight at me. I didn't need binoculars to know he was scowling.

I stared straight back. Then I reached inside for my jacket and made sure Paul got a good look at me putting it on.

He snatched his curtain closed. Now what? Did he do that so he could spy on me without my seeing him?

Just in case, I took my time closing the window, then changed my mind and opened it again. But I didn't close my curtain.

Shelly and I left the building a few minutes later. But while we were walking toward the car, I told Shelly I'd forgotten my wallet.

"Go sit in the car and wait for me," I said. "I'll run back and get my money."

She gave me her apartment key and I took my time

getting to the door. When I got upstairs, I leaned close to my bedroom window again so that Paul could see me. I really had left my wallet in my room, and I nearly forgot it for real that time because I was so anxious that Paul be aware of our leaving. I couldn't tell a thing by his windows.

When I left the building for the second time, I stopped and retied one of my sneakers. I looked up and down the block. I stopped by the big flower bed to admire the roses. I dawdled and poked along until Shelly called out, "Hey, are we going or are we not going?"

Great, I thought. Maybe Paul heard her.

"I'm coming, I'm coming!" I called back.

When we drove away, I was sure that the only way Paul—or anyone else in both apartment buildings—could not know we were going somewhere would be if he were stone dead.

All through lunch I tried not to worry about John D. But I worried anyway. If something bad happened to him, it would be my fault. I'd been really stupid and selfish, involving him the way I had.

Part of me wanted to tell Shelly that I was tired or sick—or anything!—and wanted to go home. I needed to find out what was happening across the street from our place. But another part of me wanted to stay away long enough for John D. to find out whatever he could.

Of course, maybe Paul hadn't followed us. While Shelly was driving I'd looked behind us for his car, but I couldn't be sure he was there. How many gray compact cars were there in Seattle? Thousands, maybe.

In the outdoor café, I made sure I sat facing the street, and I watched as carefully as I could. Once I thought I saw Paul driving by in a gray car, but it wasn't him.

I had pretty much given up by the time we were finishing our desserts. The plan wasn't going to work because Paul hadn't followed us and John D. couldn't get in his apartment.

And then, there he was. He was nearly half a block away, sitting on a bench at a bus stop, pretending to read a newspaper. Oh, it was him all right, even though he was wearing glasses and a hat and that stupid overcoat that looked like it belonged to a much larger man.

I pretended I hadn't seen him, but I choked on a mouthful of chocolate cake.

"Take a sip of water," Shelly advised.

I tried, but I went on choking. Everybody in the café was staring at me.

Shelly got up and patted my back. I coughed and felt better.

"Thanks," I said.

While she was sitting down, I took a quick look down the block. Paul wasn't there anymore, and I couldn't see him anywhere.

He's getting his car, I thought. He knows we're almost finished, and he's going to follow us.

"Are you feeling up to doing a little shopping again?" I asked. "I could use a pair of sandals, ones like yours, if you remember where you got them."

"Sure," she said. "Are you ready to leave?"

"Let me finish my water," I said. "I've been thirsty all morning."

I took my time draining my glass, in case Paul had parked on another block and had a long way to go. I even went to the restroom.

Finally I couldn't stall any longer. I paid the check and we walked down the street to the place where Shelly had parked.

Paul was across the street, driving slowly past us. Fortunately Shelly didn't see him.

We drove to a shoe store Shelly liked, which was a good half-hour drive away. I made myself look straight ahead and tried not to worry about whether or not Paul was following us.

John D., I thought, you'd better be finished looking through Paul's apartment, because I don't know how long he's going to stick with us when we're obviously not doing anything he could be jealous about.

We got home late in the afternoon, carrying with us two sandwiches and a green salad we'd picked up at Shelly's favorite deli. We'd had so much to eat at lunch that neither of us was especially hungry for dinner.

"I'd better check in with Eloise," Shelly said.

I could see the red light on the answering machine blinking again. Shelly pushed the Play button before she made her call.

John D.'s voice announced, "Hey, Kate, give me a call as soon as you get home."

"Remember you're baby-sitting Molly tonight," Shelly said. "Unless you've changed your mind."

"No, no," I said. "John D. probably just wants to make some plans for tomorrow."

"He sure likes you," Shelly said, and she grinned.

I blushed. Good grief, I hadn't thought about John D. in that way. But I knew Anne, my friend at home, would think he was cute and lots of fun. I hadn't had time or peace of mind enough to look at him in any way except as a source of help and information.

"I'll call him before I go over to Molly's," I said, and I shot down the hall before Shelly could say anything else about him.

I waited for what seemed like a million years, until after we ate our sandwiches and Shelly was changing clothes in her bedroom before I called John D.

"What did you find out?" I asked as soon as he answered the phone.

"Lots of stuff," John D. said. "You won't believe it. Can you meet me halfway to the park?"

"No, I'm babysitting Molly tonight," I said.

"Then I'll come over and tell you after you put the monster to bed. You need to hear this stuff, Kate."

"Tell me now," I said.

"I'm not alone," he said. "Mom and Dad are sitting out on the deck. If they come in . . ."

"Tell me what you can," I said quickly. "Before Shelly comes out of her room."

"Okay," John D. said. "First of all, you guys shouldn't ever leave the lights on when the curtain over the dining room window is pulled back. I could see your front door! He can tell whenever you leave and come home. And listen—this is spooky—he's got photos of Shelly all over his living room walls. They look like snapshots he took when she didn't know it. Shelly's never looking at the camera. There's even one of her and Eloise in the park—I recognized the statue of the bear. And there are three boxes of papers in the bedroom, old letters and different kinds of legal forms I couldn't figure out. But they seemed to have something to do with a place called Pine Hollow. Kate! That's a mental hospital!''

I sucked in my breath.

"And," John D. went on, whispering, "there's a scrapbook full of snapshots of a woman called Susan Westing, and a lot of newspaper clippings about her. She was killed in a hit-and-run accident five years ago. The driver wasn't caught. And there was a folder of letters from a lawyer. I read some of them. This lawyer kept saying that Paul's father, this Alvin King, agreed to pay Paul's expenses if he kept out of trouble, but if he didn't, his father would cut him off. And the lawyer said Paul can't go to his father's house or his office unless he's invited, and he can't phone him or write to him.''

I barely heard the last things John D. said because I got hung up on the scrapbook.

"Do you think he killed that Susan?" I asked. I was watching the hall, where Shelly would pop up any second.

"Yes!" John D. said. "I bet his father found out and made him go to that hospital.''

"That's horrible," I said.

"Kate," John D. said. "Listen to me. That Susan looked so much like Shelly that . . .''

Shelly had come up behind me. "It's time we left," she said.

I practically jumped out of my skin. "Gotta go," I told John D., and I hung up the phone.

I had to do something! I had to tell somebody about this!

But I'd better be sure of what I was doing before I started. It didn't take much imagination to see how much trouble John D. could get into because of what he'd done for me.

"How do I look?" Shelly asked. She wore a black linen suit that showed off her gorgeous blond hair. Any man would think she was beautiful.

Even crazy Paul.

He'd better not follow her tonight, I thought.

"You look gorgeous," I said. I took a deep breath and tried to act as if I wasn't terrified. "Is Eloise driving tonight? Is she going to pick you up in front of the building?"

"No, she never leaves her car on the street in front. I'll go down to the parking lot with her."

Yes, of course, I thought, furious with myself for sounding like an idiot. How else would they do it?

"I wish you were going with Andy," I blurted. "Two women alone—maybe it's not safe."

She stared at me. "Hey, what's wrong? Eloise and I have gone out lots of times at night. Why are you worrying about me?"

I couldn't meet her gaze anymore. "I don't know," I said vaguely. "I guess it makes me nervous—you and Eloise going somewhere at night."

"Kate, for heaven's sake," Shelly said. "We use common sense. We don't take any chances."

"Wouldn't you worry about me?" I asked.

"I'll worry about you being alone in Molly's apartment with her," she said. "That's what big sisters are supposed to do. Worry."

I swallowed hard. "It's what little sisters are supposed to do, too, you know," I said. "Take care of yourself, okay? I mean, you know how awful Paul is. What if he decided to follow you and Eloise to the concert? What would you do? He's really mad at the two of you. And he doesn't seem to mind making big scenes in public. Remember the day I got here?"

Before she could answer, someone knocked on the door.

I was making myself so nervous that the sound caused me to jump.

But then I heard Molly yell, "Kate, hurry up! It's almost time for "Famous Animals" to come on TV. Come on, come on!"

Shelly opened the door and Molly rushed in and grabbed my hand. "Come on, Kate, quick! You'll miss the beginning of the show!"

"I guess you know who's boss," Shelly said, laughing. "Don't worry about us, Kate. We'll be back early. And I'll call you at Eloise's during intermission. Okay?"

I nodded, but I wondered how it would be possible not to worry about her.

Not after John D. had found the newspaper clippings about the hit-and-run victim called Susan Westing.

Chapter Twelve

In Molly's apartment, we settled down quickly to watch the TV program she liked so much. But I had trouble concentrating on it. I needed to think of a way to learn what she knew about Paul. Certainly John D. and I knew enough about him now to be sure that he had hurt me and intended to do worse to Shelly. But, unfortunately, what we knew either made me sound crazy or it would get John D. in serious trouble. I was hoping that Molly had a secret that would give us what we needed and could actually use.

When the program was over, Molly demanded ice cream immediately. I went out to their kitchen—and saw that the window was bare. Anybody on the third floor across the street could see in if the light was on, and I needed to have light. It wasn't dark outside yet, but this apartment, like Shelly's, had small windows and was gloomy. But I decided I'd better do without it. The idea of Paul seeing me here gave me goose-bumps.

"Gee, doesn't it bother your mother not to have a curtain or a shade?" I asked Molly, who had followed me to the kitchen and was climbing up on a stool.

"She says anybody who looks in the kitchen window deserves the shock," she said. She gestured

151

around. "We aren't very good housekeepers."

She was right about that. It took me a while to find clean bowls for the ice cream.

"Doesn't she hate it that Paul can look in?" I asked.

"She makes faces and hopes he sees," Molly said. She didn't look too happy about it. "But we've got curtains on the other windows."

"You think she ought to worry more about him, right?" I asked. I put her chocolate ice cream down in front of her.

"Yeah, sure," Molly said. She picked up the bowl and went back to the living room.

I went right after her and tried to look casual as I closed the curtain and turned on the light. "You and I know that your mother and my sister ought to be careful around him, right?"

"Right," Molly said. She picked up the remote control and changed TV channels. She seemed nervous.

I ate half my ice cream before I spoke again. "I'm always afraid I'll run into him somewhere," I said. "I'd hate to be alone when he's around."

No response. Molly finished her ice cream and scraped the bowl. Then she started changing channels again.

"Okay, okay," I said. "I can see you don't want to tell me anything. But how will I know where not to go if you don't clue me in? You know Paul better than I do. I don't want any more trouble with him. What do you think?"

"I think you shouldn't go in the park," Molly said. Click, click, went the remote. Molly pretended to have a great interest in a politician making a speech.

"It's a nice park," I said. "Did you go there by yourself?"

Molly shook her head slowly, watching the screen. "Mom said I can't ever go there by myself."

"I bet she told you never to go out on the ledge, too," I said. "But John D. said you put his radio out there."

Molly grinned. "Yeah," she said. "Yeah."

"So have you ever been to the park alone?" I asked.

"No!" she said sharply, and she scowled at me. "I was with Mom and Shelly."

Click, click went the remote. Molly watched a cop-and-robber chase scene.

"And Paul was rude to them?" I asked.

She shook her head. "They didn't even know he was there. But I saw him by the hedge when I was playing on the swings. And that's all I can tell you. That's all!"

"Your mom doesn't want you talking about it, right?" I asked.

The look Molly gave me would have struck anybody else dead. But I was determined to find out what she knew.

"Mom doesn't know about it!" Molly said. "I didn't tell her because . . . I didn't tell her."

I shivered. "Paul made you promise not to," I said. She didn't answer.

I took a deep breath. "Molly, what did he do to you?"

She looked hard at me. "Nothing. He could never do anything to me because I'd run away."

Suddenly, in a flash, I remembered the photo John D. had talked about, the one that showed Shelly and Eloise in the park by the statue of the bear.

I picked up the TV Guide and pretended to read. "Isn't there a statue of a bear in the park? John D. said it's nice. Maybe I'll walk over tomorrow and look at it."

"If you stand on the bench, you can touch the bear's nose," Molly said.

"I'll remember that," I said. I turned a couple of pages. "Were Shelly and your mom sitting on the bench?"

"Where else would they sit?" Molly asked.

"They could have been sitting on the swings with you," I said.

"They're too old," Molly said.

I went on as if I hadn't heard her. "If they'd been sitting on the swings with you, then Paul wouldn't have bothered you."

"He didn't bother me," Molly said.

She wasn't going any farther with that idea.

I shrugged. "I only wanted to know what I should watch out for," I said.

"Don't go up and ask him any questions," Molly said. Click, click went the remote.

"Like you did?" I asked.

She nodded.

"Well, that could make crazy old Paul pretty mad," I said. "He probably thought you were spying on him. I guess we shouldn't do stuff like that."

"He was spying on them first!" Molly said. "He was taking pictures of them."

"Oh, that," I said. "I already know about that." I tried to pretend I was losing interest.

"Well, you'd better not let him find out you know, because you'll get in trouble with him," Molly said.

I had her attention now. "I'm already in trouble with him," I said, and I made myself laugh. "What else can he do?"

She stared hard at the TV. "Maybe he'll hurt Shelly to make you sorry."

I didn't say anything. I sat there like a stone. So that's what happened. Paul threatened to do something to her mother if she told anyone she'd caught him spying on them and taking snapshots.

Click, click went the remote. The screen turned black.

"Hey!" Molly said.

"You must have pushed the power button," I said. Molly pushed the power button on the remote several times, but the TV didn't go on.

"Let me try," I said. I pushed. No luck.

"I'll try to turn it back on manually," I said, and I knelt in front of the TV. But no matter what I tried, the TV stayed off.

"We can go to your place and watch," Molly said.

"I don't think that's a good idea," I said. "Your mom wants you to go to bed pretty soon. And they're going to call here during intermission. If we don't answer the phone, they'll come home to find out what's wrong."

"I know how to work the answering machine," Molly said. "We can put a message on that tells where we'll be."

I still wasn't enthusiastic about her plan. "I don't

know," I said slowly. "I've got a hunch your mother won't like the idea of you staying up so late."

"I can go to bed at your place," she said. "*After* I watch TV."

I couldn't think of a good reason to turn her down. "Okay, get your pajamas," I said. "But if there's any trouble over this, I'm blaming everything on you."

"Hey," she said. "Who else?"

While she collected her pajamas, I closed the thin curtain in the living room. Paul's windows were all dark.

Molly hadn't been exaggerating when she said she knew how to work the answering machine. She pushed a couple of buttons and then said, "Molly and Kate are in Shelly's apartment. Please call there if you want them."

"I hope your mom isn't going to be mad," I said.

"She won't care," she said. "Come on, let's go."

"You'd better not change your mind about this," I said. "I don't have a key to let you back into your apartment."

"Shelly does," Molly said. "It's in her kitchen drawer. We lock ourselves out a lot."

I opened Shelly's door and turned on the lights. Molly didn't waste an instant, but ran to the TV set and turned it on.

"Oh, good," she said. "We didn't miss much of this."

"You know, for a kid whose mother works in a bookstore, you sure watch a lot of TV," I said as I turned on the kitchen light and pulled the curtain closed. "I'm going to have a glass of orange soda. Do you want some?"

"Sure," Molly said.

We drank our sodas while we watched another program about animals. Molly yawned a couple of times, and I suggested she get ready for bed.

"In a minute," she said. She yawned again.

I went to my room, which was stuffy again, opened the window, and closed the curtain. Molly's mother would probably take her home when they returned from the concert, I thought. Otherwise, I'd be sleeping on the couch that night.

When I got back to the living room, Molly was asleep, stretched out on the couch.

Now what? I wondered.

I decided to leave her there, for a while, at least. It was possible she'd wake up on her own, and she could get ready for bed then. Meanwhile, I'd call John D. and see if he could talk. I wanted to know if he'd told me everything about his visit to Paul's apartment.

I'd use the phone in Shelly's bedroom, I decided. That way I wouldn't wake up Molly.

But the line was dead.

I sat on the edge of Shelly's bed, holding the phone, and trying to think of what could have caused the problem. I hated the feeling that swept over me, that helpless, lost-in-the-dark feeling.

What if Shelly tried to call? Would she hear a busy signal, or would the phone go on ringing? What would she think?

Maybe we should go back to Molly's place and wait for the call there, unless it was too late. Shelly might have already tried to phone. She'd be worried sick.

I had started back to the living room when I saw the hall closet door swing open.

Paul stepped out.

He was wearing black sweats and a black knit cap. Every freckle on his face stood out on his pale skin.

I was so startled that I couldn't move. I just stood there, with my mouth open.

"We have a few things to straighten out," he said. He closed the door behind him. "You haven't taken the advice I've given you, so now you'll have to pay for your mistakes."

Molly sat up on the couch. "What are you doing here?" she cried.

He didn't answer her, but spoke to me instead.

"You aren't as smart as you think you are," he said. "The brat is nothing more than an irritation. She won't stop anything. You know what has to be done and why."

Molly and I had to get out of there, but I wasn't sure how I could manage it. Paul moved two steps and stood in front of the front door, blocking us from leaving. The phone line was dead. I had to do something!

"I don't want to be here," Molly said as she got to her feet. "I want my mother."

"Run down to my bedroom, Molly," I said quickly. I was afraid of what would happen if she got close to him. He wouldn't let her out.

"Stay here," Paul snapped at her.

"She doesn't know anything about your problems with me," I said. "Go on, Molly. Hurry. Go down to my room and close the door."

She raised her gaze and stared at me.

I clenched my fists so hard my fingernails cut into my palms. "You can listen to John D.'s radio," I said. "Go on!"

She ran past Paul and down the hall. When I heard the door slam, I hoped she knew what I wanted her to do. Once she was on the ledge, she'd be out of Paul's easy reach, and maybe he'd never find out where she was. Maybe somebody would see her up there and call the police.

Maybe everything would be all right.

"She won't be able to help you, even if she sneaks into your sister's room. I cut the base lines on the phones five minutes after you left."

"How did you get in?" I asked.

He dangled a key fastened to a plastic tag with the word MASTER on it. John D. hadn't been the only one to take advantage of the lazy custodian.

"I've had this one for months." Paul smiled, showing teeth that were faintly yellow.

"You've been in here before," I stuttered.

"Stop doing that!" he yelled. "I hate listening to you, you freak. Don't do anything to make me nervous, because when I get nervous, I hurt people. Understand? I said, do you understand?"

I nodded. My knees were shaking so much that I was afraid I'd fall down. Molly, are you out of my bedroom yet? Are you safe? Does anybody see you?

"You've made me mad enough by bringing that brat over here. I didn't expect that. First it was going to be you and then your sister. And then . . . and then . . ."

He cocked his head, as if he'd heard something.

"Somebody in this building has birds," he said. "I can hear them."

I heard them, too. But they were here, in the room where we stood. I heard them cry and flutter. I felt their wings brush my head.

The only room in the apartment that had a lock was the bathroom. But if I managed to reach it, he'd be able to break the door down. If I had any chance at all, it would be out on the ledge with Molly.

But I didn't have that much courage!

"Who has the birds?" he said sharply. "I hate that racket."

"If you've got a master key, can't you find out for yourself?" I asked unsteadily.

"I told you to quit stuttering! Can't you take orders?"

He was working himself up into a rage, almost as if he enjoyed it. He was going to hurt me, I knew it, long before Shelly got home. And when she came . . .

I panicked and ran so suddenly that I surprised myself as much as Paul. I flashed past him in an instant, running down the hall to my bedroom. I fumbled with the knob, then got the door open.

The room was cold. The window stood open all the way.

I slammed the door immediately, and ran across the room. I didn't hesitate, but scrambled over the windowsill.

The street seemed miles away. No one was in sight. For a moment I wavered. I was so dizzy and so frightened that I was certain I'd fall if I tried to stand up on the ledge. But it was too narrow for me to crawl, so I had no choice. I stood up and took a step, then another. I passed the open window.

Several feet ahead, I saw Molly on the ledge, clutching ivy with both hands. It was too dark to see the expression on her face, but I was certain she was as frightened as I was.

I crept closer to her. "Molly, can you hear me?" I whispered.

"Kate!" she said. "Is he coming?"

I knew he was. I could hear him in my bedroom, stumbling in the dark. As soon as he turned on the light, he'd see the open window and know where we'd gone. If I didn't move farther along, he'd be able to reach out and grab me.

Or push me off.

"Keep going, Molly," I whispered. "Don't stop there. Keep going until you reach a window, and then start pounding on it. Yell for help."

I crept along the ledge toward Molly. She wasn't moving.

"You have to move!" I said urgently.

I glanced behind me, at the same instant the light in my bedroom flared on.

He'd know now. He'd see the room was empty.

I took two quick side steps, staring straight across the street because I was too terrified to look down. Why wasn't someone in Paul's building looking out? Should Molly and I scream? Would someone see me before Paul climbed out and pushed me off to shut me up?

I could feel the ivy now. Was it strong enough to hold me if I grabbed it?

I couldn't take the chance. I wobbled another couple of steps, and now I was close enough to Molly . . .

"Kate! Kate! Kate!"

Paul's yells almost sent me tumbling off the ledge. Now I heard birds again, shrieking wildly. Molly began crying.

"Molly, you've got to move!" I cried.

She took several quick steps, paused, and then took several more. She must be near a window.

"Can you reach a window? Knock on it!"

She didn't answer, and I didn't hear her knocking on a window either.

Paul was halfway out the window, still yelling my name. Someone must have heard him! I couldn't believe that no one was looking out the windows across the street.

I moved toward Molly. "Help us!" I screamed. "Somebody, call the police! Help us!"

A light went on across the street. At the same time, I heard Molly pounding on a window and shouting, "Open up! Open up!"

But I was in even more danger than before, because Paul was edging steadily toward me, his back to the building.

He had stopped yelling my name.

The ledge was covered with ivy, and I wasn't certain of my footing, but I didn't dare slow down. Paul was moving much faster now, and was almost close enough to touch me.

Oh, please, somebody help me, somebody help me. *I'll kill you for what you did. Kill you. Kill you.*

I stumbled a little, caught myself, and pushed on, going as fast as I dared.

Paul swung out his hand and brushed my arm. The birds shrieked.

No, no. I couldn't let him grab me.

Molly moved farther along, and pounded on another window. Across the street, a man yelled, "What's going on over there?"

Paul touched my arm again. I flinched, sidestepped, and nearly fell.

The birds beat their wings around me and then suddenly they left me and shot toward Paul.

Oh, please, let him fall. Let the birds push him. Push him.

I remembered the wall I had learned to build to shut Paul's voice away from me. I threw it up again, higher, higher, while the birds screamed and reeled.

Then, in my mind, I threw myself against that wall with all my strength, saw it topple, saw it fall, saw it hit him.

"No!" he screamed as he lost his balance.

Yes, I screamed in my mind as I pushed him over the edge.

He was gone.

I nearly fell again then, but at the last moment I clutched the ivy behind me. I heard Molly talking to someone. A man said, "Come on, now, you can make it."

"But Kate's still out there," Molly cried.

"We'll get her, too," the man said.

Across the street, a woman shouted, "The police are coming!"

That's when I finally started to cry.

At the man's urging, I felt my way along the ledge until he could reach me. The whole time I was certain

I'd fall and die, and when at last I felt his strong hand grab me, I asked, "Did Molly make it?"

"She's right here," the man said. "Take one more step. That's it. Now I've got you. Climb in."

I scrambled over the windowsill and blinked in the strong light. An elderly woman hugged me and the man who had helped me patted my shoulder.

"Kate?" Molly asked,

I looked over at her. She held something up.

"Here's John D.'s dumb radio," she said. "It doesn't work anymore."

My parents left for Seattle as soon as Shelly called them. I didn't argue about her making the call, because all I wanted was to see them again, and then pack my bag and go with them. I was more than willing to sleep in a tent or an ancient, awful hotel full of big spiders.

Two weeks later, everybody went to the airport to see us off. Shelly cried, because she refused to believe no one was blaming her for what had happened.

"You'll never come back," she said to me.

"Not as long as you live in that building," I said truthfully. "If you move, I'll come see you next summer. Okay?"

"But won't you come and see me?" Molly asked. "I live there, too."

"Not for long, kiddo," Eloise said. "John C.'s got a house for rent, and we're first on his list."

John D. had been hanging around my dad, and now I heard Dad telling him he wouldn't forget to send him the snapshot of the thousand-year-old man who got accidentally mummified in the cellar of the building where Mom and Dad had been staying.

Wonderful.

I wouldn't let myself think about that last terrible night—and Paul—until the plane took off and soared away over Seattle.

I'd been having strange dreams of a place with white walls outside and green walls inside. A place made up of small rooms with heavy metal mesh over the windows.

In one of those rooms, a man with pale tan eyes dreamed of running free again on dark streets, padding by houses where sleepers woke with a start and cried out. And the shadow he cast grew short when he ran under a street light and stretched out ahead of him after he passed it.

The shadow stretched out far enough to touch me.

Or another girl somewhere.

I knew Paul hadn't died. No matter what we were told, I knew he was still alive, in that place where his rich father kept him.

But who would believe me if I told them I had dreamed that the runner was coming once more—and the things I dream come true?

≈TERRIFYING TALES OF≈
SPINE-TINGLING SUSPENSE

THE MAN WHO WAS POE   Avi
71192-3/ $4.50 US/ $6.50 Can

DYING TO KNOW   Jeff Hammer
76143-2/ $3.50 US/ $4.50 Can

NIGHT CRIES   Barbara Steiner
76990-5/ $3.50 US/ $4.25 Can

CHAIN LETTER   Christopher Pike
89968-X/ $3.99 US/ $5.50 Can

THE EXECUTIONER   Jay Bennett
79160-9/ $4.50 US/ $5.99 Can

THE LAST LULLABY   Jesse Osburn
77317-1/ $3.99 US/ $4.99 Can

THE DREAMSTALKER   Barbara Steiner
76611-6/ $3.50 US/ $4.25 Can